# Twisted Mary
## The Beginning of The End

# Twisted Mary
## The Beginning of The End

BY

TRACY WILSON

http://beautifulpublications.com

Published by
Beautiful Publications LLC
Stratford, CT 06614

**PRINT ISBN: 978-1-7331792-4-9**
**EBOOK ISBN: 978-1-7334002-4-4**

Printed in the United States of America

# Dedication

I dedicate this series to all the women that were given second chances and smart enough to take them.

Published by
Beautiful Publications LLC
Stratford, CT 06614

**PRINT ISBN: 978-1-7331792-4-9**
**EBOOK ISBN: 978-1-7334002-4-4**

Printed in the United States of America

# Dedication

I dedicate this series to all the women that were given second chances and smart enough to take them.

# Chapter 1

"Uh uh – le'me stop you right there!" Chandler snapped... "This here – we're not doing this – this not what we came her for..."

"I understand that Chandler – but Beautiee needs to understand that she's not the grandmother – I am – and my grandchild will not be calling her son Jay..."

"Mommy! Stop it!"

"Really Mary?" Beautiee asked... "You can't let them have their moment?"

"Mary – I'ma need you to understand something quick – this is our child – not yours – not theirs – and my child will call his uncle Jay, Jay – 'cause that's his name – until his parent's change it – understand?"

"Not if I'm around he won't..."

"Starr – I know that's your mother – but if this how she's gonna act – then she doesn't have to be around..."

"Chandler – you can't stop me from seeing my grandchild..."

"Mommy!" Starr said as she started crying...

"Mary – what is wrong with you? Why would you do that to her?" Beautiee asked as she got up to hug Starr...

"Oh my – you're concern is so convenient..." I said...

"Chandler – please – can you get the waitress? I need coffee for this..." Beautiee laughed...

"May I take your orders?" the waitress asked as she came over with a pot of coffee and 5 mugs...

"Yes – we'll start with this pot of coffee – I'm gonna need more than one cup..." Beautiee said as she took the pot and poured everyone a cup...

"None for me thank you..." I said. Beautiee ignored me and poured it anyway... "I said none for me!" I snapped...

"Its fine – I'll drink it – damn!" Beautiee said...

"Can we order some food – please?" Bazil laughed...

"Sure..." Chandler answered... "Honey – no offense – just bring us some of everything on the breakfast menu..."

"Everything?" the waitress asked...

"Everything... Chandler answered...

"Okay sir – coming right up..." she said as she walked away to place our order...

"Chandler – thank you for breakfast – Mary – just what the fuck is your problem?" Beautiee asked...

"You're acting all concerned and fake – you weren't being so nice when you put Starr out the other day…" I answered…

"See – this the shit I'm talkin' about – Mary – we didn't come here for this!" Chandler snapped…

"Naa… let a Bitch talk Chandler…" Beautiee laughed as she finished her coffee. Bazil sat there drinking his coffee and shaking his head. Chandler threw up his hands…

"For starters – don't call me a Bitch – Bitch!"

"Okay…" Beautiee laughed… "What else you got?"

"I don't like you cursing at my daughter!"

"Starr…" Beautiee said as she turned to her… "Fuck and Ass are very much a part of my vocabulary – if I offended you in any way when I spoke to you – I'm sorry…"

"That's okay Beautiee…"

"Personally I thought you'd be more upset at your mother calling you a Lil' Bitch – but since I'm just your father's baby momma – I guess that ain't none of my business…"

"I'm sorry Beautiee – I shouldn't've said that to you – Chandler told me I was wrong…"

"Thank you Chandler for defending me – but Starr is right – I'm just her father's baby momma – I'm not her mother – my mistake was treating you like you were my daughter – I won't make that mistake again…"

"Beautiee – please don't say that – I love you…"

3

"I love you too Starr – that won't change..."

"Oh please – you can miss me with the cumbia bullshit – when you were in labor I helped your ass deliver your son – now you wanna act like you don't know who the fuck I am!" I snapped...

"Yes Mary – you certainly did help me – here's a gift certificate to the Classic Nails and Day Spa at Trumbull Mall to repay you for your kindness..." Beautiee said as she handed me an envelope... "Are we done now – or is there something else we need to discuss?"

"Well – now that you mention it – why were you so adamant that I couldn't be invited to your baby shower?"

"I'm so glad you asked me that..." Beautiee said as she picked up a corn muffin, buttered it, and started eating it... "Our friends are throwing us a baby shower to celebrate the birth of our son – they're not throwing us a celebration of baby mommas – personally – I'd rather not have a shower to celebrate the fact that we both have a child with my husband – what would we be doing anyway – taking a trip down memory lane – comparing notes as to who sucked my husband's dick the longest?"

"Beautiee!" Chandler yelled...

"What?" Beautiee asked as the people at the next table looked on...

"Starr's sitting here!"

"Oh please – if she ain't suckin' dick already – she's Bazil's daughter – she will be –

are we done now Mary or is there something else you need to address?"

"Actually – there is something else..." I said...

"What is it Mary?"

"Jermoll told me what he did to you – I'm so sorry that happened..." Chandler looked at Bazil and got the answer to his question without even asking as the waitress brought the food to the table...

"Bazil – I can't do this anymore..." Beautiee said as she got up from the table and ran out the restaurant.

# Chapter 2

"Waaaaaaaaa!" Jay screamed...

"Troy? Why's he cryin' like that?"

"I'on know!"

"Well he was fine a minute ago..."

"I know!"

"C'mere Jay..." Keisha said as she tried to console him...

"Waaaaaaaaa!"

"Jay... we were doing so good... calm down..."

"Le'me try Keisha..." Troy said as he took Jay and started pacing back and forth..."

"Waaaaaaaaa!"

"C'mon Jay – what's wrong?" he said as he rubbed Jay's back and Jay started to calm down a little but still cried...

"Maybe he's hungry..." Keisha said as she answered the phone... "Hello?"

"Keisha..." Bazil cried...

"Oh my God – Bazil – what happened?"

"I can't find her..."

"Who?"

"Beautiee..."

"What the fuck happened?"

"She ran out the restaurant..."

"Okay – clam down – you know she's not leaving Jay..."

"How's he doing?"

"He was fine – he just started screaming a few minutes ago..."

"He knows his mother's upset..."

"Troy got him – he's crying – but at least he stopped screaming..."

"I need to find Beautiee..."

"I'll call Beautiee – you come get Jay..."

"Okay – I'm on my way..."

"What happened Keisha?"

"Shit went left – Beautiee ran out – Bazil can't find her..."

"Oh shit!"

"Waaaaaaaaa!"

"Calm down Jay – Daddy's comin'" Keisha said as Troy rubbed his back... "I'ma call Beautiee..." Keisha said as she dialed Beautiee's cell...

"Hello?"

"Beautiee – where are you?"

"I'm home..." Beautiee cried...

"Oh thank God – Bazil's on his way here..."

"Okay..."

"You want me to come over?"

"Yea..."

"Keisha?"

"Yea?"

"You got any blunts?"

"Hell yea – you want me to bring you one?"

"Yea... and bring wine..."

"That bad huh?"

"We'll talk when you get here..."

"Okay – you want me to tell Bazil you're home?"

"Yea..."

"Okay..." she said as she hung up and Bazil came in the door...

"Waaaaaaaaa!     Waaaaaaaaa!" Jay screamed...

"Jay... Daddy's here..." Bazil said as he took Jay from Troy..."

"Waaaaaaaaa!" Jay screamed...

"Beautiee's home..." Keisha said...

"Thank you God..." Bazil said out loud...

"You're welcome..." God said...

"I'm going over there – I'll see y'all later..." Keisha said as she got up, took a bottle of wine out the fridge, grabbed her pocket book, and left...

"Troy – hand me a bottle..." Bazil said...

"Aiight – here..." Troy said as he handed Bazil the bottle...

"Okay Jay – work with Daddy – this is new to me..." Bazil laughed...

"Are you serious?" Troy laughed...

"Beautiee's breast-feeding – this is the first time he's had a bottle..."

"Oh wow!  How's he taking it?"

"He's holding it in his mouth - like a pacifier – once he tastes his mother's milk he'll drink it..."

"Bazil – what happened?"

"Fuckin' Bitch!"

"Mary – right?"

8

"Yea..."

"Beautiee was right not to bring him..." Troy said...

"She was - Chandler invited us to breakfast to tell us they're pregnant..."

"Bazil! Congratulations! That's what's up!"

"Thank you..." Bazil said as Jay finished his bottle and fell asleep...

"So – what'd you have for breakfast?"

"We didn't get a chance to have anything but coffee..."

"What the fuck happened?"

"I was so happy I cried..."

"Aww..."

"Beautiee congratulated Mary and Mary felt she needed to establish some ground rules..."

"What the fuck?"

"Chandler tried to tell her we weren't there for that but Mary said Beautiee needs to understand that she's the grandmother and her grandchild will not be calling our son Jay..."

"Yo – who the fuck she think she's talkin' too? It's not her child!"

"Chandler told Mary it's his child and his child will call our son Uncle Jay – unless we change that..."

"What the fuck she say to that?"

"She said not when she's around – and Chandler told Starr if that's how your mother's gonna act – she won't be around – Starr started crying... and Beautiee got up to comfort her..."

"That's fucked up..."

"Exactly – so the waitress comes over with a pot of coffee – Beautiee takes the pot, pours us all coffee – Mary gets mad because Beautiee poured her coffee and she didn't want any..."

"What the fuck is wrong with her?"

"Me..."

"What?"

"She wants me... and I don't want her..."

"Damn..."

"So I ask if we can order some food – so Chandler tells the waitress to bring some of everything from the breakfast menu..."

"Damn – and y'all didn't even get to eat..."

"So Beautiee asked Mary what the fuck her problem was..."

"I know that's right – what she say?"

"Chandler said we weren't there for that but Beautiee said let a Bitch talk..."

"Haa haa!"

"She got mad – said don't call her a Bitch – then called Beautiee a Bitch..."

"Oh shit!"

"Beautiee said okay – what else you got? And Mary brought up the other day when we put Starr out..."

"Oh damn..."

"She said she didn't like Beautiee cursing at her daughter..."

"Beautiee cursed at her?"

"Beautiee said get your ass and no-the-fuck you're not..."

"Oh shit – I thought she cursed Starr out..."

"Beautiee would never do that – but she apologized anyway – and she told Starr I thought you were more offended when your mother called you a Lil' Bitch – but since I'm just your father's baby momma I guess that ain't none of my business..."

"Oh shit!"

"Starr apologized for saying that but Beautiee told her she was right – she made a mistake by treating her like she was her daughter and she wouldn't make that mistake again..."

"Oh shit! What did Starr say?"

"Starr apologized and told Beautiee she loves her and Beautiee said I love you too – that will never change..."

"Oh shit – that's not like Beautiee..."

"So Mary says miss her with the cumbia shit because she helped Beautiee when she was in labor and now Beautiee wanna act like she don't know who the fuck she is..."

"Yo – I can't – is she serious?" Troy laughed...

"So wait..." Bazil laughs... "Beautiee gives her a gift certificate to the spa at Trumbull Mall and says here – to repay your kindness – are we done now – or do you have something else?"

"Yo – your wife is gangasta!" Troy laughed...

"So now Mary wants to know why she couldn't be invited to the baby shower..."

"Yo! What the fuck? She ain't invited! Who the fuck she think she is?"

"Wait..." Bazil laughed... "Beautiee told her it's a baby shower – not a celebration of baby mommas – she didn't want a shower to celebrate that they both have a child by me – and then she asked her..." Bazil couldn't stop laughing...

"What Bazil – what?"

"She asked her – what would they do – go down memory lane and compare notes as to who sucked my dick the longest!"

"Aaaaahhaaaaa! Aaaaahhaaaaa!" they both laughed...

"Chandler got mad and said Starr's sitting here – Beautiee said oh please – if she ain't suckin' dick already she's Bazil's daughter – she will be..."

"Oh shitttt!" Troy laughed... "Yo! I love Beautiee!"

"I love her too..."

"Wait... what happened?"

"When Beautiee was in prison..." Bazil said as he started crying...

"Bazil... give me the baby..."

"No... I need to hold my son..."

"What happened?"

"Beautiee was sexually harassed by one of the officers..."

"Damn... I'm sorry..."

"She didn't report it... but I found out... and I paid him a visit..."

"Oh shit..." Troy whispered...

"I followed him into the bathroom... I reached in his pants... I took his dick and his balls in my hand..."

"I would'a ripped them off!" Troy snapped...

"The only reason he left with his dick attached... is because he didn't rape my wife..."

"Okay – I'm confused – what does this have to do with Mary?"

"He told Mary what he did to my wife..."

"Wait – what?!"

"And she told Starr... and Chandler..."

"This morning? At the restaurant?"

"Yes..."

"Fuckin' Bitch!"

"I swear – if it wasn't for my son and my wife – I'd kill her..."

"Oh shit – Chandler didn't know!"

"And Mary knew it..."

"Beautiee – where are you?"

"I'm in the kitchen..."

"Girl – what happened?" Keisha asked as Beautiee started crying...

"We not talkin' about nothin' until we smoke a blunt..."

"Okay..." Keisha said as she lit the blunt, took a pull, and passed it to Beautiee...

"Damn..." Beautiee said as she took a pull and started choking...

"Damn Beautiee..." Keisha laughed... "How long has it been?" she laughed again as she took another pull and passed it back to Beautiee...

"Too long..." Beautiee laughed as she took another pull and it went down smooth...

"Hol' up – gimmie my shit!" Keisha laughed...

"You brought more than one – right?" Beautiee laughed...

"Yea..."

"Well – light it!" Beautiee laughed. Keisha lit the blunt and started smoking it...

"You not gonna share?" Beautiee laughed...

"You can finish that one – this here – is mine!" Keisha laughed...

"Shit – I'm hungry – I need somethin' to eat..."

"Didn't you just have breakfast?"

"No..."

"Fuck you mean no?"

"No..." Beautiee said as she went in the refrigerator, took out the bread, eggs, cheese, and bologna...

"You sure you can cook?" Keisha laughed...

"No..." Beautiee laughed as she put the frying pan on the stove and turned the flame on low...

"Whatchu makin?"

"I'ma try to make a fried bologna, egg, and cheese sandwich..." Beautiee laughed...

"Well... try and make me one too..." Keisha laughed as she opened the bottle of wine, poured two glasses, and spilled the rest... "Oh shit..." Keisha laughed... "Sorry..."

"Don't worry about it – the counter was thirsty... Ahhaaaa!"

"Oh shit – turn the flame down..." Keisha laughed...

"Its fine – this is how my mother used to do it – see... the... bubble..." Beautiee laughed as she took the fried bologna out the frying pan, put it on the bread, and then cracked the eggs into the frying pan...

"Don't burn the eggs..."

"I'm not!" Beautiee laughed...

"Le'me see..." Keisha laughed as she watched Beautiee flip the eggs over...

"I told you – I won't burn them..." Beautiee laughed. Once the eggs were done, Beautiee put the cheese on the eggs and turned off the fire under the frying pan. When it was melted, she put the egg and cheese on top of the bologna, put the slice of bread on top, and handed the sandwich to Keisha...

"Okay – its aiight – I still can't believe you went to Cracker Barrel and didn't eat..."

"I didn't..." Beautiee said as she ate her sandwich...

"Why though?" Keisha asked as she drank her wine..."

"Because Keisha... shit went left..."

"I hate that Bitch..."

"So do I..."

"Somebody needs to fuckin' take her ass out..."

"Somebody will..."

"Oh shit – le'me stop..." Keisha laughed as Bazil came in with Jay...

"Hey Jay – come to Mommy!" Beautiee said as she tried to get up and fell back in the chair...

"Oh shit – Beautiee's fucked up!" Keisha laughed...

"That I am, that I am!" Beautiee laughed as she put her finger up in the air...

"Beautiee – let me take Jay upstairs – then I'll come get you..."

"Bazil – I wanna see Jay..."

"I don't think that's a good idea right now..."

"Bazil! Bring me my son!"

"Okay..." Bazil said as he brought Jay over to Beautiee...

"Hey Jay – Mommy loves you..." Beautiee said as she kissed him on the forehead...

"I'ma take him upstairs – then I'll come get you – okay?"

"That's fine..." Beautiee laughed... "Who's gonna get Keisha?"

"I'on need nobody to get me – I can walk home – it's only next door!" Keisha laughed...

"Wait here – I'll be right back..." Bazil said as he took Jay upstairs and called Troy...

"Hello? Beautiee's okay?"

"She's high – and so is your wife..."

"Oh shit – they lit?" Troy laughed...

"Yes..." Bazil laughed...

"I'll be right there..." Troy laughed as he hung up. As soon as Keisha saw Troy, she said... "Whatchu call him for – I can walk – Beautiee's the one fallin' n shit!" she laughed...

"C'mon Keisha – let's go home..." Troy laughed...

"I'm aiight Troy..." Keisha said as she stood up... and stumbled...

"C'mon – I gotchu..." Troy said as he held on to her waist and walked her out...

"You so romantic..." Keisha said as they both left...

"What's this?" Bazil asked...

"Keisha spilled wine..."

"I see – you cooked something?"

"I'm sorry..."

"For what?"

"I didn't make you a sandwich..."

"That's okay... I'll get something..." he said as he pulled Beautiee up out the chair and held her...

"I love you..."

"I love you too..." he said as he walked her out the kitchen towards the stairs...

"Let's go upstairs..." Beautiee said...

"We are..." Bazil said as he picked her up, put her over his shoulder, and carried her upstairs. When they got to the top of the stairs, he put her down, walked her into the bedroom, and laid her down on the bed...

"I'm sorry..."

"You have nothing to be sorry for..." Bazil said as he kissed her and she fell asleep...

# Chapter 3

"Mommy! Whhhyyyyy!" Starr cried...

"I'm sorry... it's just..."

"Shut the hell up Mary – matter fact – leave!" Chandler snapped as he comforted Starr...

"How the hell am I supposed to get home?"

"Take an Uber to the mall and get the coastal link!"

"You can't give me a ride?"

"I could – but I'm not!"

"It's always my fault..." I mumbled under my breath...

"It is your fault!" Starr screamed...

"Starr... calm down..." Chandler said...

"No! Now I know why you never wanted me to contact Daddy – you didn't give a damn about me – all you ever cared about was yourself!"

"Starr – don't you talk to me like that!"

"Why not? 'Cause its true? Daddy doesn't want you Mommy – he loves Beautiee – get over it!"

"Starr... stop..." Chandler said...

"No! We came here to celebrate our having a baby and you can't even be happy for me because you're so busy being miserable! C'mon Chandler – I wanna go see my father..."

"Yes Starr - run to your father – to hell with your mother right?" I asked...

"Fine by me!"

"Starr! That's your mother!" Chandler snapped...

"Don't remind me!" she snapped back... "Beautiee hasn't done anything but try to be nice to you – but that's not enough for you – Chandler's right – you don't have to be around our child!"

"Try and stop me..." my mother said. Chandler got up and left the table as we continued...

"You know what Mommy? Good luck paying the expenses on the co-op – I'm not helping you anymore!"

"Where the hell am I supposed to get the money?"

"Get a job!"

"You know I can't get a job – I'm a felon!"

"I'll call Ms. Crystal – Social Services has programs to help felons that just got out of prison find work – and she can give you an application for cash, food stamps – and especially – my rent!"

"Your rent? Please – what are you gonna do – evict your mother?" I asked as Chandler came back to the table with the manager...

"That's exactly what I'm going to do!" Starr screamed...

"Is this the lady?" the manager asked as he pointed me...

"Yes sir…" Chandler answered…

"Sorry for the inconvenience Sergeant – Maam – I'm afraid I need to ask you to leave…" the manager said…

"Chandler? You're having me thrown out by the manager?" I yelled…

"Leave with him – or get arrested by them…" Chandler answered as he pointed to the approaching officers…"

"Fine – I'll leave – but this isn't over…" I snapped as I stormed off…

"Yes it is…" Chandler said as he pulled Starr into a hug and kissed her… and she started crying…

"Uh uh – stop that…" Chandler said as he kissed her eyes, her tears, and her mouth…

"Can we go see my father?"

"We can try…"

"Sir – would you like us to wrap this up for you?" the manager asked…

"Yes please…"

"Okay – we'll get right on that for you…" he said as he snapped his finger for the waitress to wrap up the food. Once the food was wrapped and bagged, Chandler went to pay the check but the manager stopped him…

"Sir – it's on us – we want you to come back – tell all the officers in your precinct when they come for breakfast the coffee's on us!"

"Okay – thank ya sir – where's our waitress?"

"I'll get her for you…" the manager said as he went to get her…

"Is there a problem sir?" the waitress asked...

"Here Honey..." Chandler said as he handed her a $100 bill...

"Thank you!" she beamed...

"You're welcome..." Chandler said as they took the bags and headed out to the car. Starr waited for Chandler to open the door for her and then she put the bag in the front seat, sat down, and started crying again...

"Starr... please don't cry..." Chandler whispered as he started tearing up...

"I can't help it Chandler..."

"Let's go tell Jay he's gonna be an Uncle..."

"Okay..." she said as Chandler started the car and they drove to her father's house. When they got there Chandler parked the car and then he spoke...

"Wait here – I'ma go get Keisha and Troy – we'll use them to get in the house..." Chandler laughed...

"Good idea..." Starr laughed as Chandler closed the door and went to get them...

"Who is it?" Troy asked...

"It's Chandler..."

"What's up Chandler?" Troy asked as he opened the door...

"I need your help..."

"What happened?"

"Starr wants to see her father but I don't think Bazil will let us in – but he might open the door for you and Keisha..."

"Okay – le'me see if I can wake her up – come in..." Troy said as Chandler stepped inside...

"Keisha..." Troy whispered as he woke her...

"Huh?"

"Chandler's downstairs..."

"Oh... that's nice... tell him I said hi..." she said as she turned over...

"Keisha..."

"What Troy?"

"He wants to go see Bazil..."

"Okay..."

"Keisha..."

"Yes Troy – what?"

"He wants us to go knock on the door for him..."

"Are you fuckin' serious?"

"He said if he knocks on the door Bazil might not let him in..."

"Damn – I still don't know what happened..." Keisha said as she got up... "All I know is Beautiee said they didn't eat and shit went left..."

"C'mon Keisha – let's go – maybe she'll tell you later..."

"Do you know what happened?"

"Yea..."

"So you can tell me then..."

"No Keisha... I can't..."

"Damn Troy – was it that bad?"

"Yea..."

"You right – Bazil won't let them in – let's go..." she said as they came downstairs... "Hey Chandler..."

"Hey Keisha – thanks y'all..." Chandler said as they closed the door and went to her father's house...

"Okay – we'll knock on the door – y'all be quiet..." Troy said as Chandler and Starr took the bags out the car and went up to the door...

"Who is it?" Bazil asked...

"It's Troy..."

"Hold on Troy..." Bazil said as he opened the door and saw them standing there...

"Here Dad – take this – it's heavy..." Chandler said before Bazil could say anything...

"What's this?" Bazil asked...

"Breakfast..." Chandler answered...

"From Cracker Barrel?" Keisha asked...

"Yea..." Chandler answered as they all went inside...

"Aiight – we'll see y'all later – I'm tired..." Keisha said as she turned to leave...

"Keisha – Troy – we have plenty of food – and good news – sit!" Chandler said as they all sat at the kitchen table... "I'ma put all this food on the island – y'all pick what you want to eat..." Chandler said as he put the following plates on the island:

Old timer's Breakfast
Sunrise Sampler
Grandpa's Country Fried Breakfast
Country Boy Breakfast

Smokehouse Breakfast
Country Morning Breakfast
Double Meat Breakfast
Uncle Herschel's Favorite
Grandma's Sampler – Pancakes
Momma's Pancake Breakfast
Wild Main Blueberry Pancakes
Pecan Pancakes
Buttermilk Pancakes
Buttermilk Pancakes with Fruit toppings
Momma's French Toast Breakfast
French toast
Eggs-In-The-Basket

Beautiee walked into the kitchen with Jay... "Hey Beautiee..." Chandler said. Beautiee didn't answer him – she just sat down with Jay...

"Can I hold Jay?" Starr asked. Beautiee didn't answer her either – she just got up and handed Jay to her... "Hi Jay – guess what – you're going to be an Uncle...

"For real? Y'all pregnant?" Keisha asked...

"Yes – we're pregnant..." Chandler answered...

"Congratulations! I know your mother's excited. Nobody said anything... "What? What'd I say?"

"Nothing – Mary's very excited..." Chandler said...

"Thank you for breakfast Chandler..." Troy said...

"You're welcome – c'mon y'all eat – there's plenty!" Chandler said...

"I'll take Jay so you can eat Starr..." Beautiee laughed as she took Jay...

"What's so funny?" Keisha asked...

"This morning – at the restaurant..." she laughed...

"What happened?" Keisha asked...

"Starr said I love you Daddy – Bazil said I love you too Starr - Chandler said do you love me too Daddy – she wouldn't be pregnant if it wasn't for me!"

"I know that's right!" Keisha laughed...

"Yo – that's funny as hell!" Troy laughed...

"And true!" Chandler laughed as they all got up to get plates...

"Damn this food looks good!" Troy said...

"Thank you Chandler..." Beautiee said...

"You're welcome – you're not eating?"

"I'll let Bazil eat first – he hasn't had anything to eat yet..."

"I'll take Jay Beautiee..." Starr said...

"Eat Starr – you're eating for two... or three..."

"Two? Or Three?"

"Two – you and the baby – three – you and twins..."

"Oh my God – you think I'm having twins?"

"Hmmm... you might be..."

"Aww..." Starr said as she started crying...

"Aww look – she's happy..." Keisha said...

"My favorite kinda tears..." Chandler said...

"Shit – y'all make me wanna get pregnant – all happy n shit..."

25

"Who? You?" Troy asked...

"Yea – why not?"

"Keisha..." Troy said as we walked up behind her, held her, and kissed her... "Are you serious?"

"Yea..." she said as she turned around and kissed Troy...

"Keisha... I love you..."

"I love you too..." she said and then she kissed him again...

"Beautiee – eat..." Bazil said as he came over to take Jay..."

"Okay..." she said as she picked up the Momma's French toast Breakfast and sat down to eat... "So... how's your sex life?"

"Ummm... it's fine..." Starr mumbled...

"Don't be embarrassed Starr – I have to warn you though – now that you're pregnant – you'll be on ten..."

"I will?"

"Yea – and you'll make Chandler very, very happy..."

"She already does..." Chandler said...

"That's not what I mean..." Beautiee said...

"Whatchu mean then?"

"How can I put this – okay – I got it..." Beautiee said as she put food in her mouth, chewed, and swallowed... "Starr – you'll enjoy sex – and Chandler will enjoy it more than he does now..."

"Okay – that's what I'm talkin' about!" Chandler laughed...

"Once you get pregnant – your vagina changes... for the better..."

"Aww shit – it's on and poppin' Keisha!" Troy said...

"Fuck you mean – it's already on and poppin'!" she laughed...

"I'm tellin' you – it gets better – or worse – depending how you look at it – but I don't have that problem – Bazil's ready whenever I am right Bazil?"

"Umm... yea..."

"Bazil – Starr's pregnant – she's fuckin' – it's okay to talk about sex!" Beautiee laughed...

"Beautiee?"

"Yes Starr?"

"What happens after the baby's born?"

"Your vagina stays the way it is..."

"It does? So you mean I stay on ten?"

"Yes – and Chandler will enjoy it more too..."

"Okay – I like that shit!" Chandler said...

"So... after the baby... does it hurt?"

"No Starr..."

"Even if you have all natural?"

"No Starr – it doesn't hurt..."

"How long do we have to wait?"

"The doctor will tell you to wait six weeks but if you feel okay – do you..."

"Oh – so you're still waiting 'cause Jay is only two weeks old..."

"Shit – the hell I am!" Beautiee laughed...

"You mean... you and Daddy... didn't wait?"

"Nope…"

"I hear that!" Troy said as he and Bazil high-fived…

"I talked to the doctor – he told me some of his patients get pregnant before they leave the hospital!" Bazil laughed…

"Oh that's nasty!" Keisha said…

"Not to some people…" Bazil laughed…

"I'm gonna be like you… and Chandler's gonna be like Daddy…"

"Aww shit – I'm wit it!" Chandler laughed…

"You're breast feeding – right?"

"Yes Starr…"

"Does it hurt?"

"No – you might get a little sore but you just use some cream to help with that…"

"When will I get milk?"

"You'll get milk when you're about five or six month pregnant – your breasts will swell up too – they may be tender – Chandler will need to massage them…"

"He already does that…" Starr laughed…

"No Starr – this won't be sexy – sometimes they hurt – especially when they fill up…"

"Oh – what do I do?"

"You just feed your baby – if you have twins – feed one from each breast so they won't be full…"

"Ok… okay…"

"You been to the doctor yet?"

"No…"

"Go to Dr. Julianne – she's good – she's my doctor – and she's your mother's doctor – she doesn't deliver babies so you'll need to find another one when you get further along…"

"Okay… thanks Beautiee…"

"For what?"

"For talking to me…"

"You don't have to thank me for that Starr…" Beautiee said as Bazil smiled…

"Okay y'all – I'm full – and tired – I need to lie down – and I need Troy to lay me down…" Keisha laughed…

"Okay!" Troy laughed…

"We might as well get going too…" Chandler said as he got up…

"Bye Daddy, bye Beautiee…" Starr said as she hugged them both… "Bye Jay" she said as she kissed him on the forehead…

"Bye Dad, bye Beautiee…" Chandler said as he hugged them…

"Bye y'all – congratulations…" Keisha said as she hugged them…

"Congratulations…" Troy said as he hugged them…

"Go 'head Keisha – I'll hug y'all later – I'm tired too…" Beautiee said…

"We'll talk soon…" Bazil told them as they left…

"Come here Mrs. Osgood…" Bazil said as he pulled Beautiee close to him and kissed her… "I love you so much…"

"I love you too Bazil…"

"I love how you love Starr…"

"I can't help it – I can't stay mad at her – besides – she can't help who her mother is..."

"Let's go upstairs..." Bazil said as he smiled at Beautiee mischievously...

"I'll be right up... I just need to check something on the computer real quick..." Beautiee lied...

"Okay... I'll put Jay to bed..."

"Okay... I'll be up in a minute..." Beautiee said as she went into the library and made a phone call from her cell...

"Hello..."

"How are you?"

"I'm fuckin' pissed!"

"So you've seen her?"

"I was at Cracker Barrel..."

"How soon can you make this happen?"

"How soon do you want it?"

"I want it yesterday..."

"I'll let you know when it's done..." he said and then he hung up...

"Beautiee?"

"Yes Bazil?"

"Are you coming?"

"Not yet..." she said as she started upstairs..."

"How long are you going to be?"

"That..." she said as she wrapped her arms around Bazil's neck and kissed him... "Depends on you..."

# Chapter 4

"Who is it?" Beautiee yawned as she went to answer the door...

"Keisha!"

"What's wrong?" Beautiee asked as she snatched the door open...

"That's what I came to find out..." Keisha said as she pushed her way inside...

"Ummm... come in!" Beautiee laughed...

"Who is it?" Bazil yawned...

"Hey Bazil..." Keisha answered...

"Hey Keisha – you good?"

"To be honest – no..."

"What's wrong? You need me to go get Troy?" Bazil asked...

"Actually – I need you to leave us alone so we can talk... if you don't mind..."

"Okay... I'll be upstairs with Jay..." Bazil said as he went upstairs...

"How many blunts did you bring this time?" Beautiee laughed...

"I didn't bring any..."

"Aww shit..."

"Okay – I brought one – but I'm not leaving until you tell me what happened – Troy knows what happened – he said he can't tell me – my husband and I don't keep secrets from each other – so I'ma need you to tell me what happened..." Beautiee didn't say anything. She got up and went into the library and sat down. Keisha got up, went into the library, and sat down next to Beautiee. Beautiee got up, closed the door, and locked it...

"Thank God I didn't bring my son..." Beautiee sighed...

"Why?"

"I was so nervous when we got there... I couldn't go inside right away... Bazil took me in his arms and held me until I felt better – and until Chandler saw us and yelled for us to hurry up and come inside..."

"You felt that bad?"

"Yea...when we got to the table Starr was so happy to see her father she gave him a hug right away so I said I guess I don't get one – but then she gave me one..."

"Damn – you picked up on that shit outside!"

"So I sat down next to Mary and I spoke to her – she spoke without looking up – my husband spoke to her – she spoke without looking up..."

"Just a rude Bitch!"

"So Chandler announces they're pregnant – we're so happy – we get up from the table, we hug them – Bazil started crying 'cause he was happy for them - and that's when Chandler made the joke about do you love me too Daddy – she wouldn't be pregnant if it wasn't for me..."

"Yea – that shit was funny!" Keisha laughed...

"So I'm trying to be nice to this Bitch – I say congratulations Mary – you're going to be a grandmother – this Bitch starts talkin' 'bout yes I am and now that you said that we need to establish some rules..." Keisha pulled the blunt out her purse, pulled out her lighter, lit it, took a pull, handed it to Beautiee, and Beautiee took a pull too...

"I can't..." Keisha said as she took another pull and handed it back to Beautiee...

"So Chandler tells her le'me stop you right there – we not doing this – this not what we came here for – Bitch gon' say Beautiee needs to understand that she's not the grandmother – I am and my grandchild will not be calling her son Jay – so Starr tells her mother to stop it and I said really Mary you can't let them have their moment – and Chandler tells her she need to understand that this is their child and their child will call his Uncle Jay Jay until his parents change it – the Bitch gon' say not if I'm around he won't – so Chandler says Starr I know that's your mother but if this is how she's gonna act she don't have to be around – Bitch gon' say you can't stop me from seeing my grandchild – Starr starts crying – I get up to comfort her – Bitch gon' tell me my concern is so convenient!"

"Girl – we 'bout to run out – I should'a brought three blunts – and what the fuck she mean convenient?"

"Girl – I told Chandler to get the waitress 'cause I need coffee for this – the waitress comes over with a pot of coffee and 5 mugs so I tell her we'll start with coffee – I pour everyone a cup of coffee – Bitch gets an attitude 'cause I poured her a cup of coffee and she told me she didn't want it!"

"Wai' a minute – her daughter is crying – you comfort her – she don't give a fuck about her daughter – but she's mad at you for pouring her a cup of coffee – I'm mad at you too – you should'a poured the fuckin' coffee on her got damned head!"

"So Bazil's laughing – he asks if we can order food – the waitress comes over – Chandler orders the entire menu – I say Chandler thank you for breakfast – Mary – what the fuck is your problem?"

"I know that's right! What she say?"

"She gon' say I'm acting all concerned and fake but I wasn't being so nice when I put Starr out the other day – so Chandler said we didn't come here for this – I told Chandler naa... let a Bitch talk!" Beautiee laughed...

"Yes girl!" Keisha laughed...

"So she gon' say for starters – don't call me a Bitch – Bitch – I said okay – what else you got – she gon' say I don't like you cursing at my daughter!"

"You was wrong for that Beautiee..."

"I know – and I apologized – to Starr – but I also told her personally I thought you'd be more upset at your mother calling you a Lil' Bitch – but since I'm just your father's baby momma – I guess that ain't none of my business..."

"Oh shit! She fucked up wichu..."

"She said she was sorry and Chandler told her she was wrong – I told Chandler thanks for defending me but Starr is right – I'm just her father's baby momma – I'm not her mother - my mistake was treating her like she was my daughter – I won't make that mistake again..."

"Oh shit! You meant that?"

"Yea... I did... but you know I can't stay mad at her..."

"Good..."

"So now this Bitch gon' say oh please – you can miss me with the cumbia bullshit – when you were in labor I helped your ass deliver your son – now you wanna act like you don't know who the fuck I am!"

"No she didn't!"

"Yes she did – so I gave her a gift certificate to the spa place at Trumbull Mall to repay her kindness!"

"Shit – I wouldn't 'a gave that Bitch shit!"

"So I asked her are we done or is there something else you need to address – Bitch gon' say why were you so adamant that I couldn't be invited to your baby shower?"

"First the fuck all – she wasn't throwing you a baby shower – we are – and she don't dictate a mutha fuckin' thing over here – you know what – I'ma beat that Bitch ass when I see her!"

"So I said I'm so glad you asked me that – our friends are throwing us a baby shower to celebrate the birth of our son – they're not throwing us a celebration of baby mommas – personally – I'd rather not have a shower to celebrate the fact that we both have a child with my husband – what would we be doing anyway – taking a trip down memory lane – comparing notes as to who sucked my husband's dick the longest?!" Beautiee laughed...

"Yooooo! Wait..." Keisha laughed... "I can't... you actually said that shit?"

"So Chandler gets mad talkin' bout Starr's sitting here – I said oh please – if she ain't suckin' dick already – she's Bazil's daughter – she will be – are we done now Mary or is there something else you need to address?"

"Oh God..."Keisha laughed... "I wish I was there – I would'a been on the fuckin' floor!"

"Keisha... I have something to tell you... I wish I didn't have to tell you – Bazil and I were going to keep it between us..."

"Oh shit..."

"Remember when I was in prison?"

"Yea..."

"I was sexually harassed..." Beautiee said as she started tearing up...

"Damn Beautiee..." Keisha said as she started rubbing her arm... "Did you report it?"

"No..."

"Why?"

"I didn't want to – I just wanted to come home..."

"That's fucked up – he shouldnt'a got away with that shit..."

"He didn't..."

"He didn't?"

"No..."

"You told Bazil..."

"Damn right I did..."

"Is he alive?"

"No..."

"Oh shit! Bazil killed him?"

"Keisha... if my husband had actually killed someone..."

"Never mind – he's dead – he can't do it to anybody else – wai' a minute..."

"Yes Keisha?"

"What does this have to do with Mary?"

"He was fuckin' her..."

"You lyin'!"

"He told her what he did to me..."

"Beautiee..." Keisha whispered as she took some tissues out of her purse and wiped her eyes... "That's so fucked up..."

"You haven't heard the worst..."

"Oh God... what?"

"I asked Mary if there was anything else she needed to address..."

"Beautiee – I know you not fixin' to tell me..."

"Bitch gon' say – at the table – in front of Starr and Chandler – Jermoll told me what he did to you – I'm so sorry that happened..."

"Jermoll? The officer that was killed in Trumbull Gardens?"

"Yea..."

"Chandler didn't know..."

"No..."

"So that's why you ran out the restaurant..."

"Yea..."

"So they wasn't gettin' in here yesterday if we didn't knock on the door – were they?"

"No..."

"Chandler ain't try to call y'all?"

"He might've tried to call Bazil – but he won't call me – I wouldn't speak to him about it anyway..."

"This some fucked up shit – Mary knew exactly what the fuck she was doing..."

"And now I know exactly what the fuck I have to do..."

"You goin' be alright girl..." Keisha said as she hugged Beauiee...

"I am... in a minute..."

"I love you... and I'm sorry..."

"I love you too – now go back home and start workin' on that baby..." Beautiee laughed as she unlocked the door to the library and walked Keisha towards the door...

"Shit – why you think I said I needed Troy to lay me down when I left here yesterday?" Keisha laughed...

"I hear that!" Beautiee laughed as Keisha left.

"How'd that go?" Bazil asked as he came downstairs. Beautiee didn't answer him – she just started crying as Bazil pulled her into a hug and held her.

# Chapter 5

"Hello Mary..." Wayne said as I came inside...

"Wayne?" I asked nervously... "How'd you get in here?"

"There's not a lock on earth I can't get into... especially when I have a key..." he answered as he held up the key...

"Where'd you get that?"

"Aren't you happy to see me?"

"I'm surprised..."

"Speaking of surprises... I'm surprised by a lot of things..." he said as he got up to double lock the door...

"Oh? What surprises?" I asked as I started shaking...

"Well..." he said as he came up behind me and pulled me close to him so he could breathe in my ear... "I was surprised you never tried to find me..."

"I thought you didn't want anything to do with me – with us..."

"Mary – you know I loved you – I loved you both – but you never loved me..."

"That's not true – I did love you..."

"Did you?"

"Yes..."

"Prove it..."

"Okay..." I said as I tried to undress but Wayne stopped me...

"How long were you sleeping with Bazil?"

"A few months..."

"Whose idea was it to let me raise that mutha fucka's daughter as mine?"

"Mine..."

"Why? Of all the men in the world – why him?" he asked as he turned me around to face him...

"I loved him..." I whispered as I started crying...

"You just said you loved me..."

"I did..."

"You didn't love me... you loved Bazil – you didn't gave a damn that he was married to your best friend – you wanted to have a child with him – and you used me to raise that mutha fucka's child because you wanted his child – isn't that right?"

"No... that's not true... I knew you wanted children..."

"Yes..." he said as he kissed me... "I wanted children..." he said as he held me by the throat and began squeezing...

"Please... you're hurting me..."

"Am I?"

"Yes... please..."

"Please what?"

"I can explain..."

"I'm glad you said that..." he said as he released his grip from my throat... "Make us a drink... then you can explain..."

"Okay..." I whispered as I went into the kitchen and made drinks for us...

"Need any help?" Wayne asked as he came into the kitchen...

"No... I'm okay..."

"I'll take one of the glasses for you..." he said as he took one of the glasses and went into the living room and sat down on the couch. I came into the living room and sat down next to Wayne.

"Now..." he said as he took a couple of sips... "Please explain to me... why I saw you with Jermoll..."

"Oh my God – you've been watching me?"

"Yes – I've been watching you... intently..."

"I had no idea..." I said as I finished my drink...

"So... explain... you... and Jermoll..."

"Jermoll started visiting me in my cell when I was in prison..."

"You mean he raped you..."

"No... it wasn't like that..."

"What was it like?"

"I was lonely..."

"So... even in prison... you found a way to use another man..."

"We used each other..."

"So... when you got out of prison – you were so lonely – that you turned to Jermoll – instead of looking for me?"

"Yes..."

"But you love me... right?"

"Yes..."

"So... explain to me why... you were at the Cox Law Firm?"

"Oh my God – you know about that too?"

"I told you – I've been watching you intently..."

"I was there to file a lawsuit against Bazil for back child support..."

"So... you went to file a lawsuit against Bazil for back child support – for a child I raised? Aaahhhhaaaaa! Aaahhhhaaaaa! So – how much was the lawsuit for?"

"$150,000..."

"Hot damn! We're gonna get paid!"

"No... we're not..."

"Why not?"

"Because... I dropped the lawsuit..."

"Because you love him..."

"Wayne – I don't love Bazil... not anymore..."

"So you admit you did love him?"

"Yes..."

"So... why'd you drop the lawsuit then?"

"Because... they were so nice to me – they included me in the wedding..."

"Because... you wanted to be close to Bazil..."

"That's not true..."

"Yes... it is..."

"No... it's not... I swear..."

"I saw you... at the precinct..."

"You did?"

"Yes... so... explain... what were you doing at the precinct?"

"Jermoll made me the beneficiary on his retirement benefits..."

"Why would he do that?"

"Because he loved me..."

"Did you love him?"

"He asked me to marry him – I said yes..."

"You didn't answer my question..."

"I cared about him..."

"So... you were going to marry a man you didn't love... for what – money?"

"I was going to marry a man that loved me..."

"I see – well – now that you've said that – will you marry me?"

"What?"

"I just asked you to marry me..."

"I can't..."

"Why not?  You know I love you..."

"Yes... I know that..."

"So why can't you marry me then?"

"I need more time..."

"More time to make Bazil and Beautiee's life a living hell?"

"No!"

"I saw you at Cracker Barrel..."

"Oh my God..."

"Starr's right... you can't let go of Bazil..."

"That's not true – I don't want him!"

"Prove it..."

"How?"

"You said you needed more time to accept my proposal... no time like the present..." he said as he got up and went towards the bedroom...

"Please... don't hurt me..."

"Like you hurt me?"

"I didn't mean too... I'm sorry..."

"Prove it..." Wayne said as he waited for me in the bedroom doorway...

"Okay..." I said as I went towards the bedroom. When I got to the doorway Wayne grabbed me in his arms and held me...

"I missed you..." he said as he kissed me deeply...

"You never came to see me in prison..." I said as he walked me backwards towards the bed...

"You loved Bazil the whole time you were with me – you had me raise his child – I was angry... and hurt... I'm still angry... I'm still hurt..." he said as he started undressing me...

"Starr loved you..."

"And I loved her – until I found out she was Bazil's daughter..."

"So you hate her?"

"Right now..." he said as he pushed me back on the bed... "You should be more concerned with how I feel about you..."

"I'm sorry..."

"Stop telling me you're sorry..." he said as he took off his clothes and got on the bed... "And start showing me..." he said as he lay down beside me and started massaging my breasts... "You're afraid of me..."

"Yes... I am..."

"Good..." he said as he got on top of me and spread my legs...

"Wayne... please... don't..."

"I thought you wanted a man that loves you?"

"I... I... do..."

"Well then..." he said as he moved down between my legs... "Let me show you how much I love you..."

"Oh Wayne... it's been so long..." I moaned...

"Mmmm....." Wayne moaned as he licked, sucked, and slurped on my pussy...

"Don't stop Wayne... yes... yes... just like that..." Wayne was turned on by the fact that he had me right where he wanted me and just like I wanted, he didn't stop... "Wayne... oh God..." Wayne picked me up by my ass and put his tongue inside... "Waaayyynnnneeee!" I screamed as he darted his tongue in and out my ass, alternating between sucking my ass, my pussy, and my clit... "Oh God... Wayne... Fuck!" Wayne inserted his index finger in my ass, his thumb in my pussy, and began massaging my G-spot while sucking my clit, sending me into orgasmic convulsions... "Aaahh! Aaahh! Aaahh! Aaahh!" I screamed as my body came up off the bed and my legs shook... "Wayne... shit..." I breathed but Wayne wouldn't stop... "Wayne... wait..." Wayne looked up at me and my juices glistened in the sunlight on his chin...

"I'm not done..." he growled and then he went back to sucking my clit and massaging my G-spot...

"Oooohhh... Wayne... it's too intense... I can't take it..." Wayne stopped sucking hard and flicked my clit with his tongue while continuing to massage my G-spot and I started moaning again... "Wayne... huh... Wayne..." Wayne took his thumb out my pussy, inserted another finger in my ass, and finger-fucked my ass while simultaneously licking and sucking my pussy... "Wayne... Oh shit... I'm cumming again..." Wayne continued finger-fucking my ass and started sucking my clit hard... "Waaayyyne! Aaaaahhhhh!" Wayne slowed down until my orgasm subsided and then he moved up my body, laid down on top of me, and kissed me as he eased himself inside me... "Oh Wayne..."

"Yes... Mary..." he breathed as he started thrusting...

"Fuck me... please..."

"As you wish..." he growled as he picked up my legs, put them on his shoulders, and fucked me hard...

"Wayne! Oh God! Fuck me!"

"Uggh! Uggh! Uggh! Uggh!"

"Yes! Just like that! Haaahh!"

"Whose pussy is this?"

"Yours! Oh God! Yours!"

"Damn right it's mine... Ugggghhhh!"

"I'm cumming! I'm cumming!"

"Uggh! Uggh! Uggh! Uuuugggghhhh!"
Wayne put my legs down laid down on top of me,

covered my mouth with his, put his tongue in my mouth, slid out my pussy, eased himself in my ass, and started fucking me again...

"Mmmm....    Mmmm....    Mmmm.... Mmmm...."

"Mmmph! Mmmph! Mmmph! Mmmph!"

"Mmmm....    Mmmm....    Mmmm.... Mmmm...."

Mmmph! Mmmph! Mmmph! Mmmph!" Wayne stopped kissing me and breathed in my ear... "Damn your ass is tight... uuuggh...."

"Your dick feels so good in my ass..." I breathed as I grabbed him tighter...

"Did you give my ass to anyone while I was away?"

"No..."

"Is this my ass?"

"Yes Wayne... Yes..."

"Cum for me..."

"Oh... yes... harder... right there... right there..." Wayne was happy to oblige and started fucking me harder...

"Aaaahhhhhh!"

"Ugghh! Ugghh! Ugghh! Ugghhhhhh!" Wayne collapsed on top of me and sucked my breasts as our orgasms subsided...

"Oh Wayne... I needed that..." I breathed...

"Mmmm... so did I..." he said as he sucked my breasts. I held Wayne against me as he continued sucking my breasts and Wayne didn't stop until his dick was limp and slid out my ass... "We could have this every day... if you want it..."

"I want it..." I breathed...

"So you'll marry me?"

"Yes Wayne..." I breathed as I grabbed his face and kissed him... "Yes..."

"I have a surprise for you..." Wayne said as he got up, went to his duffel bag, pulled out two passports, and sat back on the bed with me...

"What's this?" I asked as he handed the passport to me...

"Read it..."

"Oh my God! How'd you get me a passport?"

"I know a guy..."

"Where are we going?"

"I'm glad you asked me that..." Wayne said as he went back to the duffel bag, pulled out two Amtrak tickets, and gave one to me...

"Ontario? We're going to Canada?"

"Yes... if you'll come with me..."

"When will we be back?"

"We won't..."

"I'm not sure Wayne..."

"Why?"

"Starr's pregnant... I want to be in my grandchild's life..."

"What kind of like would that be Mary?"

"I don't understand..."

"I saw you at the restaurant... you were angry..."

"I had every right to be..."

"You also have a right to be happy..." Wayne said as he kissed her...

"Oh Wayne... I want to..."

"We leave on Friday – we'll leave from New York at 7:15 a.m. – we'll transfer in Niagara Falls..."

"Oh... I've always wanted to go to Niagara Falls..."

"We can spend some time there... if you like..."

"I'd like that..."

"We'll be in Ontario on Friday night..."

"Where will we live?"

"That's my other surprise..." Wayne said as he went back to his duffel bag, pulled out a laptop, and logged on to realtor.com... "Here – take a look..."

"Oh wow – Wayne – it's so cute!"

"You like it?"

"I love it – how can you afford this?"

"I used the money we embezzled from Bazil..."

"Oh wow..." I laughed...

"So... is that a yes?"

"Yes Wayne..."

"I have something else for you..." Wayne said as he went back to the duffel bag and pulled out a small velvet box...

"Wayne..." I whispered as I started crying...

"I'm going to ask you one more time..." Wayne said as he opened the box... "Will you marry me Mary?"

"Yes Wayne... Yes..." I cried as Wayne put the ring on my finger...

"You've... made... me... the... happiest... man... in... the... world..." he said between kisses...

"Oh Wayne – we're leaving Friday – there's so much to do - I need to call Starr and..." Wayne stopped me by kissing me abruptly...

"Wow..." Mary breathed...

"Don't call Starr..."

"Why?"

"I saw you at the restaurant... I heard what she said to you..."

"She has every right to be upset with me..."

"Write her a letter..."

"Write her a letter? You don't want me to say goodbye?"

"I just want you to be as happy as you are right now – with me – I've waited so long..."

"Okay – I won't call her..."

"Good..."

"Can I call her after we're married?"

"Of course..."

"When are we getting married?"

"We can go get our marriage license today – wait 48 hours – and go get married in the courthouse before we leave if you want – or we can get married in Niagara Falls – you choose..."

"I wanna get married in Bridgeport – and I want to start our honeymoon in Niagara Falls..."

"Okay – let's go get our marriage license..." Wayne said as he jumped up off the bed and started getting dressed... and I started crying...

"What's wrong?" Wayne asked as he came over to me and held her...

"I don't deserve you..." I cried...

"Uh uh..." Wayne said as he kissed me... "You deserve to be happy... say it..."

"I... deserve... to... be... happy..." I sniffed...

I'm not convinced..." Wayne said as he kissed me again...

"I deserve to be happy..." I said as I smiled...

"Damn right you do – now let's do this..." he said as he kissed me again...

"Mmmm.... Okay..." I said as I hurried up to get dressed and we both went out the door... "I can't believe we're actually doing this..."

"We are..."

"I can't wait to get to City hall..."

"Me either..." We took the bus downtown and walked hand-in-hand to City Hall. When we went inside, we went straight to the City Clerk's offce...

"Good afternoon – how may I help you?" Ms. Woody asked...

"We're here to apply for our marriage license..." Wayne answered...

"Congratulations – do you have ID?"

"Can we use our passports?" Wayne asked...

"Yes – that's fine..."

"Okay – here are your applications – fill them out, sign them, date them, give them to me, and I'll process them for you..."

"Okay..." Wayne said as he took the forms...

"Here Mary – here's one for you..." he said as he pushed the form over to me and smiled...

"Wayne?"

"Yes Mary?"

"I'm taking your name..."

"Really?"

"Yea..."

"I love you Mary..."

"I love you too Wayne..."

"Keep your name too – especially since your passport is in your maiden name..."

"Okay..."

"We're ready..." Wayne said as he took the papers from me and handed them to Ms. Woody along with his papers...

"Okay – everything is in order – I just need to ask you both a few questions – I'll start with Mary – is this your signature Mary?"

"Yes..."

"Did you complete this application of your own free will?"

"Yes..." I answered as I smiled at Wayne...

"Okay – now that you've confirmed it's your signature and you've also confirmed that you completed this application of your own free will, I'll sign it..." Ms. Woody said as she signed my application... "Okay Wayne – now it's your turn..." she said as she put Wayne's application in front of him... "Is this your signature?"

"Yes..."

"Did you complete this application of your own free will?"

"Yes I did..." Wayne answered as he smiled at me...

"Okay – now that you've confirmed it's your signature and you've also confirmed that you completed this application of your own free will, I'll sign it..." Ms. Woody said as she signed Wayne's application... "Wait here – I'm going to process the applications and I'll come back with your marriage license..." she said as she went to her office in the back...

"I'm so excited - I wish we could get married right now!" I exclaimed...

"You do?" Wayne asked...

"Yes..."

"Here's your marriage license..." Ms. Woody said as she handed the marriage license to Wayne... "Do you have any questions?"

"How long do we have to wait before we can get married?"

"Are you in a hurry?" Ms. Woody laughed...

"Yes I am..." I answered...

"Well... Connecticut doesn't impose a waiting period... so you can get married whenever you want..."

"Can we get married right now?" Mary asked...

"Right now?"

"Yes..."

"Are you serious?" Wayne asked...

"Yes... I'm serious..."

"Mary... I love you..." Wayne said as he pulled me into a deep, passionate kiss...

"I love you too..." Mary breathed...

"I'd be happy to marry you now... if you want..." Ms. Woody said...

"Okay!" I squealed...

"Alice — this couple wants to get married — come with me..." Ms. Woody said as we all followed her to the rotunda. When we all got there, Ms. Woody spoke... "Give Alice your cell phone so she can record the wedding and take pictures..."

"Okay..." Wayne said as he handed Alice his phone...

"Okay — I need you both to stand here and face each other..."

"Okay..." we both said in unison as we stood facing each other and took hands...

"Start recording Alice..."

"Okay..." Alice said...

"Beloved... we are gathered here this afternoon to join Wayne Robinson and Mary Smith in marriage. You have both come before me, expressed your desire to become husband and wife, and you're both in a hurry!" she laughed along with us. "Do you have rings?"

"Yes — we have rings..." Wayne said as he took two ring boxes out his pocket...

"How'd you know we'd need both rings today?" I asked...

"You were so happy... I had a feeling..." Wayne answered...

"Okay – take the rings out the boxes – Mary – you take his ring – Wayne – you take her ring..."

"Okay..." we both said in unison as I took his ring and he took mine...

"Okay – Wayne – do you have anything you want to say to Mary?"

"Yes I do..." Wayne answered as he took my hand... "Mary – I've loved you for many years. Today, you're making me the happiest man in the world. Thank you for loving me back..." I didn't wait for Ms. Woody to ask as I responded to Wayne...

"Wayne – you loved me even when I didn't love myself. Today – you're making me the happiest I've ever been in my life – and I know it's only going to get better from here. Thank you for not giving up on me..."

"I love you so much..." Wayne said as he kissed me...

"We're not finished..." Ms. Woody laughed...

"Sorry – I couldn't help it..." Wayne laughed...

"That's alright – now Wayne, I took it upon myself to choose your vows – repeat after me..."

"Okay – I'm ready..." Wayne said...

"Mary – I take you as my wife, with your faults and your strengths, as I offer myself to you with my faults and my strengths..." Wayne repeated after Ms. Woody and then she continued... "I will help you when you need help and turn to you when I need help. Today - I choose to spend the rest of my life with you..." I started crying as Wayne repeated the vows to me. When he was finished, I took his face in my hands and kissed him. Ms. Woody shook her head and laughed... "Okay Mary – repeat after me..."

"Okay – I'm ready..." I said...

"Wayne..." I said... and then I started crying. Wayne took his hands, touched my face, and wiped my tears before I continued... "I take you as my as my husband, with your faults and your strengths, as I offer myself to you with my faults and my strengths. I will help you when you need help and turn to you when I need help. Today – I choose to spend the rest of my life with you..."

"By the power invested in me by the State of Connecticut and the City of Bridgeport – I now pronounce you husband and wife. Wayne – you may kiss your bride!" People had already started to gather in the rotunda and everyone erupted in applause as Wayne and I held each other and kissed. "Everyone – I present to you – Mr. and Mrs. Wayne Robinson!" Ms. Woody said as the applause continued. Alice stopped recording and started taking pictures as Wayne and I hugged Ms. Woody and she hugged us back... and then she started crying...

"Aww..." Everyone said as Alice captured it in the pictures...

"How soon will we get our marriage certificate?" Wayne asked...

"You'll get it in about a week or so..."

"Can you send it to our new address?" I asked...

'Is it here in Bridgeport?"

"No – it's in Ontario..." I answered...

"You're moving to Canada? When?"

"Friday..."

"I won't be able to get it to you by then – but if you give me your new address I'll make sure Vital Records sends it there..."

"Thank you Ms. Woody..." I said...

"Please – call me Alberta..."

"Thank you Alberta..." I said...

"Yes Alberta – thank you..." Wayne said...

"You're welcome – now go get your phone from Alice – congratulations..." she said as she hugged us both, Alice gave Wayne his phone, and we left City Hall.

# Chapter 6

"Where would you like to go now?" Wayne asked...

"I want to go get a room at the Holiday Inn and make love to my husband..." I answered...

"Okay – we can definitely do that – are you hungry?"

"Yes... I'm hungry..."

"You wanna go eat at Thelma's?"

"No..."

"You don't like their food?"

"I do – I just want to be alone... with you..."

"Okay – we can go straight to the hotel then..." Wayne said as he took me by the hand and we walked hand-in-hand to the hotel.

"Welcome to the Holiday Inn Bridgeport – how may I help you?"

"We'd like a room for tonight..." Wayne said as he pulled me to him and held me...

"Hmmm... let me see what I can do..." the clerk said as she went on her computer...

"It looks like you're in luck – we have two rooms left – both with a king size bed – is that okay?"

"That's fine!" I answered...

"Okay…" the clerk laughed… "Will that be cash, check, or charge?"

"Cash…" Wayne answered…

"Okay – that'll be $171.00 – that's $149.00 for the room, taxes, and surcharges…"

"Here…" Wayne said as he gave the clerk $200.00…

"Thank you – will the room be in your name?" the clerk asked…

"Can you make it in both names?" I asked…

"Sure – what are your names?"

"Wayne & Mary Robinson!" I beamed…

"Okay! May I have your address?"

"201 East Arrow Highway, Toronto, Ontario M1E4Y1…" Wayne answered…

"Wow – you're a long way from home!" the clerk exclaimed…

"Yes we are…" I said as the clerk entered our information…

"May I have an email address for our records?"

"WayneRobinson12@gmail.com" Wayne answered…

"Would you like me to email a copy of this to your email?"

"Yes please…" Wayne answered…

"Okay – here's your room keys – the pool is located upstairs – your room is down here on the first floor – room 115 – it's the last room on your right…"

"Thank you…" Wayne said as he took the keys, put them in his pocket, took me by the hand, and led me down the hall. When we got to the room he took the key out his pocket and handed it to me..." I want you to open the door..." he said after he picked me up in his arms...

"Oh Wayne..." I sighed and opened the door...

"Welcome to the first day of the rest of your life Mrs. Robinson..." Wayne said as he carried me into the room and stood me up..."

"I'm Mrs. Robinson..." I cried...

"Yes..." Wayne said as he took my face in his hands, and kissed me... "You're Mrs. Robinson..."

"I'm nervous..."

"Why?"

"It's my wedding day..."

"You don't have to be nervous..."

"I can't help it..."

"We already know we're sexually compatible..." Wayne said as he started kissing my neck...

"Ooohhh... my husband is kissing his wife on her neck..."

"Yes... yes I am..." he said as he pushed me down on the bed...

"Wayne... wait..."

"Why?" he breathed as he kissed his way down to my breasts..."

"I'm hungry..."

"So am I..."

"I need to eat..." Wayne stopped kissing on me, propped himself up on his elbow, and looked at me...

"Mary – what's wrong?"

"I just need to eat..."

"Is that all?"

"I haven't had anything to eat... and I haven't had any coffee..."

"Okay – I'll make you a cup of coffee from the coffee maker – and we'll order burgers and fries off the menu – okay?"

"Okay..."

"I love you... Mrs. Robinson..." he said as he kissed me...

"I love you too... Mr. Robinson..." Wayne got up to make coffee and I sat up on the bed... "Wayne?"

"Yes Mary?"

"We should order something besides burgers and fries..."

"What would you like?"

"Steak – or seafood – and champagne..."

"We'll toast in our hotel glasses..." Wayne laughed...

"Maybe they have champagne glasses..."

"Maybe..."

"Our first cup of coffee as husband and wife..." I sighed as Wayne gave me my coffee...

"When I woke up this morning – I never thought I'd be drinking coffee with my wife this afternoon..." Wayne said as he sipped his coffee...

"I was scared when I saw you..."

"I know..."

"I thought you wanted to hurt me..."

"I didn't want to hurt you – I wanted you to choose me – and you did..."

"I have a confession to make..."

"You don't need to do that Mary..."

"I want to..."

"Okay..."

"When I finally admitted to you I loved Bazil... that was the first time I ever acknowledge it to anyone else..."

"Really?"

"Yes..."

"Who else did you admit it to?"

"Starr..."

"What made you finally admit it to me?"

"I hurt you... and you still wanted me... I owed you the truth..."

"Wow..."

"I still don't believe I deserve to be happy..."

"Why?"

"Because... I was sleeping with my best friend's husband..."

"Mary?"

"Yes Wayne?"

"You still feel that way? Even now?"

"Actually... now that we're married – I'm starting to believe I deserve to be happy..."

"Good – 'cause I wouldn't want to have to spank you..."

"What if I want a spanking?"

"Do you?"

"Well... I have been a little naughty..."

"Yes... you have..." Wayne said as he finished his coffee and looked at the room service menu... "They have steak, potatoes, and vegetables and they have seafood pasta – which one – oh never mind – I remember..." Wayne said as he picked up the phone to order room service...

"Hello?"

"Yes – I'd like to order room service – I'd like the steak – well done – and the seafood pasta... yes – I'd like a bottle of champagne... you have glasses? Great... about 45 minutes? Okay..." Wayne said as he hung up...

"Go sit on the edge of the bed – never mind – come sit in this chair – and bring a pillow with you..." I said...

"Okay..." Wayne said as he took a pillow off the bed, came over to the chair, and sat down... "Why do I need a pillow?"

"It's not for you... it's for me..." I said as I put the pillow on the floor in front of him, kneeled on it, and unbuckled Wayne's pants. Wayne looked down at me as I took his dick out and put it in my mouth...

"Mary..." Wayne moaned as I took his dick all the way in my mouth, pulled it back out, took it all the way back in my mouth, and pulled it back out again... "Mary... shit..."

"You like that Daddy?"

"Hell yea..." Wayne breathed as I took his dick back in my mouth again and started sucking it... "Oh... Mary... Fuck..." I wrapped my hand around the base of his dick and moved my hand up and down as I continued sucking his dick...

"Mary... oohh... ooohhh... Mary..." I squeezed his dick and continued moving my hand up and down as I sucked his dick harder... "Mary... I'm cumming! Uuuggghhh!" he moaned as he rose up out the chair and I swallowed every drop... "C'mere..." Wayne breathed as he took my face in his hands, pulled me up, and kissed me hard... "Now..." he said before kissing me again... "Get your ass on the bed..."

"We don't have time – the food..."

"I said..." Wayne said as he kissed me again... "Get your ass on the bed..." I sat down on the bed. Wayne walked over to me, pushed me down on the bed, and unzipped my pants. After he unzipped them, he pulled them down along with my panties to my ankles, took them off, picked up my left leg, and began kissing me up my leg...

"Ooohhh..." Wayne continued kissing me up my leg until he reached my pussy, and then he spread my lips with his tongue... "Wayne..." I whispered as I lifted my ass up off the bed...

"Ssshhh..." he said as he spread my legs wide and dove in...

"Waayynnneee!"

"I told you... ssshhh..." he said ad then he started flicking his tongue on my clit. I grabbed a pillow and bit into it...

"Mmmmm!"

"Uh uh..." Wayne said as he took the pillow away from me... "That's cheating..." and then he went back to flicking his tongue on my clit...

"Mmmm….. Mmmmm…. Mmmm……" I moaned as I bit my bottom lip…

"You just can't be quiet…"

"I can't help it…"

"And I can't help but punish you…" Wayne said as he stood up… "Turn around… get on your knees, and grab the headboard…"

"Okay…" I breathed as I did as I was told…

"Now…" Wayne said as he eased himself inside me… "I'm going to spank you… for being naughty…" he said as he grabbed me by my hips and started fucking me…

"Wayne… oh God…"

"Smack!"

"Yes! Fuck me!"

"Smack!"

"Harder!" Wayne obliged me by fucking me harder as he continued smacking my ass…

"Oh God… Fuck me… I'm cumming!" I screamed. Wayne grabbed my hips with both hands and fucker me hard as I bucked back against him until my orgasm subsided and I began to slow down, but didn't stop…

"You don't want me to stop… do you?"

"No…"

"Say it…"

"Please… don't stop…"

"I won't… I'll fuck you… as long as I want to…" he growled and then he grabbed my hips and started fucking me hard again…

"Wayne! Fuck!"

"Uggh! Uggh! Uggh! Uggh!"

"Ohh... Ohh... Ohh.... Ohh..."

"Uggh! Uggh! Uggh! Uuuugggghhhh!"

"Aaahh...      Aaahhh...      Aaahhh... Aaaahhhh!"

"Room service!"

"Be right there..." Wayne laughed as he got up to answer the door and I collapsed on top of the bed and covered my ass with a pillow. Wayne opened the door and smiled as the waiter smiled back at him... "I know you heard us..." Wayne said as he took the tray inside the room and stepped out into the hallway...

"I did..." the waiter acknowledged as he put his head down...

"Uh uh – don't be embarrassed..." Wayne said as he took the check, signed it, and tapped the waiter on his chest...

"Okay... thank you sir..." the waiter said as he took the check and went down the hall. When Wayne went back in the room I spoke...

"He heard us – didn't he?"

"Yes... he did..."

"Oh my God – I'm so embarrassed!"

"Why?"

"Because..."

"Mary – what do you think people do in hotel rooms?" Wayne laughed...

"They fuck..." I sighed...

"Damn right they do – now come sit – let's eat..."

"Okay..." I said as she went to put my pants back on...

"Uh uh – leave 'em off – I'm not done with you yet..." he said as he smiled at me mischievously...

"Okay..." I smiled as I sat down at the table... "Take off your pants..." I said as I smiled at Wayne mischievously. Wayne got up, took his pants off, and walked over to me... "Oh my..." I breathed...

"You like what you see?"

"Very much..."

"Good..." he said as he went to sit back down and I peeked under the table. Wayne slid down in the chair and opened his legs to give me a better view and I smiled.

"Spread your legs..." he said. I slid down in the chair and spread my legs so Wayne could see... "Let's eat..." Wayne said as he uncovered the dishes...

"Ooohhh... this looks so good..." I breathed. Wayne picked up the bottle of champagne, popped the cork, poured two glasses, and put the bottle to his mouth...

"Aaahhh... good..." he said as he passed the bottle to me...

"Oh... yes..." I breathed as some of the champagne dribbled out of my mouth...

"I guess you got a hole in your mouth..." Wayne laughed...

"I guess I do..." I laughed as I put the bottle down...

"Let's toast..." Wayne said as he picked up his glass...

"Wayne... wait..."

"Ummm... okay..."

"Take my hands..."

"Sure..." Wane said as he took my hands, I closed my eyes, and prayed...

"Lord – I'm not sure what I did to deserve this – but thank you..."

"You're welcome..." God said...

"Mary..." Wayne whispered with tears in his eyes... "Did you just thank God... for me?"

"Yes..." Wayne got up, came over to me, pulled me up out the chair, and held me...

"Nobody's ever been thankful for me – I love you so much..."

"I love you too..."

"Thank you God for bringing me back to my wife..."

"You're welcome..." God said...

"Let's toast!" Wayne said as he picked up the glasses and handed one to me...

"To my husband..." I said as we both sipped...

"To my wife..." Wayne said as we both sipped... "and... to Beautiee..." Wayne said as he sipped but I didn't..."

"Did you just toast to Beautiee?"

"Yes..."

"Why?"

"Drink Mary..." I sipped my champagne reluctantly and sat down... "I can explain..." Wayne said as he sat down...

"Okay..."

"Let's start eating – here – try some steak..." he said as he put a piece of steak in my mouth...

"It's good..." I said and then I started eating my seafood pasta...

"Beautiee found me in facebook..."

"In facebook?"

"Yes..." he answered as he put some food in his mouth, chewed, and swallowed... "She asked me to come to you..."

"Why? Why would she do that?"

"To be honest... she thought if we got back together..."

"What?"

"You'd be happy..."

"I was happy!"

"Mary?"

"Yes Wayne?"

"Tell me the truth..."

"Sigh... I wasn't really happy..."

"Exactly..."

"How long have you been in contact with her?"

"For a few weeks..."

"So... if it wasn't for Beautiee reaching out to you... you wouldn't be here?"

"I don't know – I didn't think you wanted me..."

"I'm sorry..."

"I know..."

"But you came anyway..."

"I had to... I needed to know one way or the other..."

"I don't know whether to be mad at Beautiee... or thank her..." I laughed...

"My turn to confess..."

"Okay..."

"I've been miserable without you too..."

"Oh Wayne..." I said as I got up, went over to Wayne, sat in his lap, took his face in my hands, and kissed him. Wayne held me tight and thrust his tongue in my mouth...

"Mmmph..."

"Hmmph..."

"Mmmph..."

"Hmmph..."

"Let's finish eating... so we can have dessert..."

"Okay..." I said as I picked up the phone...

"Front desk..."

"Yes – I'd like a later check out please..."

'Okay Mrs. Robinson – you're all set – your check out time is now 12 p.m.tomorrow afternoon..."

"Thank you..." I said as I hung up and went to sit back down. Wayne smiled at me and we finished our food without speaking. I stood up, took of my shirt and my bra, and stood in front of Wayne with my hands on my hips. Wayne stood up, took his shirt off, tossed it in the chair, and stood in front of me. I smiled at Wayne as he walked towards me, fully erect, pressed his erection up against me, and held me... "You feel so good..." I whispered..."

"So do you..." Wayne whispered as he walked me backwards towards the bed. Wayne took down the spread, the sheet, and the blanket – and then he got in the bed and patted the spot next to him for me to join him. I got in the bed next to him and Wayne pulled me to him, thrust his tongue in my mouth, got on top of me, and eased himself inside me before I had a chance to react. I spread my legs wider and grabbed his ass with both hands, indicating to Wayne that I was ready, and we continued tonguing each other down as he started making love to me again... "Mmmph... Mmmph... Mmmph... Mmmph..."

"Hmmph... Hmmph... Hmmph... Hmmph..." I dug my nails into Wayne's ass, indicating to Wayne that I wanted it harder, and Wayne held my legs up by my thighs, and happily obliged me...

"Mmmph... Mmmph... Mmmph... Mmmph..."

"Hmmph... Hmmph... Hmmph... Hmmph..." Wayne stopped, pulled out, flipped me over, eased himself back inside me, and continued...

"Uggh... Ugghh... Ugghh... Ugghh..."

"Huuhh... Huuhh... Huuhh... Huuhh..."

"How you like it Mommy?" he growled in my ear...

"I love it Daddy!" I moaned...

"How you want it?"

"Anyway you give it to me..."

"Mmmm... I like that..."

"Huuhh... Huuhh... Huuhh... Huuhh..."

"Yes Mommy... That's it... Enjoy it..."

"Fuck me Daddy!" Wayne pulled out of me, wrapped his arms underneath me, pulled me up on my knees, held me, and eased himself in my ass... "Oh yes Daddy... yes..."

"Got damn!" Wayne moaned as he fucked my ass...

"Oh God... Wayne... Fuck me..."

"Ugghh... Ugghh... Ugghh... Ugghh..."

"Haah... Haah... Haah... Haah...

"Ugghh... Ugghh... Ugghh... Ugghh..."

"Wayne... I'm cumming! I'm cumming!"

"Ugghh... Ugghh... Ugghh... Ugghh..."

"Aaagh! Aaagh! Aaagh! Aaaaggghhhh!"

"Ugghh... Ugghh... Ugghh... Uuuugggghh!" Wayne slowed down, laid on my back, held me, and continued fucking me until my legs stopped shaking and I collapsed on my stomach...

"Oh my God..." I breathed. Wayne kissed my neck and bit my ear lobe as his dick went limp in my ass and his cum ran down my leg onto the bed. Wayne got up, flipped me over on my back, laid down on top of me, and kissed me... "I had no idea it was gonna be this good..." I breathed as I held Wayne...

"Neither did I..." Wayne breathed and then he kissed me again...

"Let's finish the champagne..."

"Okay..." Wayne said as he got up, got the bottle of champagne, got back in the bed, pulled up the covers, took a swig, and handed the bottle to me...

"I don't wanna check out..." I breathed and then I took a swig of champagne and handed the bottle back to Wayne...

"We have to..." Wayne said as he took a swig and handed the bottle back to me...

"I know..." I said as I finished the champagne and put the empty bottle on the night stand... "I just wish we didn't have to..."

"I'll give it to you just as good no matter where we are..." Wayne said as he pulled me down onto my back and got on top of me...

"Mmmm... that sounds good..." I breathed...

"Let's get some sleep..." Wayne said as he kissed me..." and I'll give you some more before we check out..."

"Okay..." Mary yawned...

"Good night Mrs. Robinson..." Wayne said as he kissed me again...

"Good night... Mr. Robinson..." I yawned as we both drifted off to sleep.

# Chapter 7

Wayne opened one eye and looked at his phone vibrating on the nightstand... "Who the hell is calling me at 7 a.m.?" he whispered as he picked up his phone to answer it... "Hello?"

"Good morning..."

"Hang on a sec..." Wayne said as he got up and went into the bathroom...

"Are you peeing right now?" Beautiee laughed...

"As a matter-of-fact..." Wayne laughed... "I am..."

"Where are you?"

"I'm with my wife..." he whispered...

"Your wife? You got married?"

"Yes..."

"I underestimated you..."

"I told you I'd take care of her..."

"Congratulations..."

"Thank you... even if you don't really mean it..."

"I mean it Wayne..."

"You do? Why?"

"Because I know you really love her..."

"I do..."

"Does Starr know?"

"Not yet – but don't tell her..."

"It's not my business – she'll hear it from her mother..."

"Thank you..."

"So when did you get married?"

"Yesterday..."

"Oh wow! I'm impressed!"

"So was she..."

"Damn – it went down? Like that?"

"Let's just say you were right..." Wayne laughed...

"When are you leaving?"

"Friday morning..."

"Oh my God – I can't wait!"

"I'll keep you posted..." Wayne whispered as he hung up. Wayne left the bathroom, put the cell phone on the nightstand, and called room service...

"Good morning – may I help you?"

"Yes – I'd like to order breakfast for two..." Wayne whispered...

"How would you like the eggs?"

"Scrambled..."

"Will that be white, wheat, rye, or an English muffin?"

"White..."

"Bacon or sausage?"

"Bacon..."

"Orange juice?"

"Yes..."

"Coffee?"

"Yes..."

"Okay – about 30 minutes..." Wayne got back in bed and kissed me awake...

"Good morning..." I yawned...

"Good morning..."

"What time it is?"

"It's a little after 7..."

"Why are we up so early?"

"I order breakfast..."

"Thank you..." I said as I got up and went to the bathroom. When I came out the bathroom I got back in bed, pulled up the covers, and turned over...

"Ummm... Mrs. Robinson?"

"Yes Mr. Robinson?"

"Are you turning your back on me?"

"I'm sorry... I'm tired..." Wayne got in bed next to me and put me on my back...

"Mrs. Robinson?"

"Yes Mr. Robinson?"

"I need you to get ready for breakfast..." Wayne said as he kissed me...

"Please... I'm tired..."

"I'll let you sleep at home..." he said as he kissed me again...

"Can't I just lay here until the food comes?"

"Sure... you can lay there... if you want..." Wayne said as he sucked on my right breast...

"Ooohhh..." Wayne continued sucking on the right breast and began playing with the left one...

"Ooohhh..." Wayne got up on top of me, spread my legs, slid down between them, and started licking my clit...

"Ooohhh..."

"Yes Mommy... feed me..."

"Oh Wayne..." Wayne stuck his tongue inside my pussy and started sucking...

"Wayne! Huuhh! Huuhh!" I was getting wetter and Wayne was relentless as he licked, sucked, and slurped...

"Huuhh! Huuhh! Huuhh!" Wayne stuck three fingers in my pussy and finger-fucked me as he sucked my clit hard...

"Wayne! Aaagh! Aaagh! Aaagh!" I was thrashing back and forth as I clenched the bedspread with my fists and my body shook... "Waaaayyynnnneeee!" I screamed as I came and my body rose up off the bed...

"Mmmm...." Wayne moaned as he licked, sucked, and slurped until I stopped shaking...

"Wayne..." I whispered. Wayne moved up between my legs, lay on top of me, and stuck his tongue in my mouth... "Mmmm...." I moaned as we lay there kissing...

"Room service!"

"Be right there!" Wayne said as he got up to put on a robe and answer the door...

"Good morning Mr. Robinson – shall I bring this inside for you?"

"No thank you – I'll bring it in..." Wayne said as he signed the check and handed it to the waiter...

"Thank you – enjoy your breakfast..." the waiter said as he went down the hall. Wayne wheeled the table into the room and sat down in front of it. I got up and sat at the table...

"Coffee Mrs. Robinson?"

"Yes Mr. Robinson…" Wayne made us both a cup of coffee with sugar and cream and I spoke… "I can't believe I'm sitting here having breakfast with my husband…"

"You are…" Wayne said as he lifted the covers off the plates…

"Ooohhh… this looks so good!" I said as I started eating…

"I'm glad you're so happy…"

"I am…"

"I know…" Wayne said as he started eating… "So when are you going to tell Starr we're married?"

"Part of me wants to scream it from the rooftop…"

"And the other part of you?"

"Wayne…" I said as I touched his hand…

"Yes Mary?"

"You left her…"

"I know…"

"That hurt…"

"I know…"

"I want to see her… but…"

"You don't know if she'll want to see me?"

"Yea…"

"She has a right to be angry… she has a right to be hurt too…"

"Can you accept that from her?"

"I have to… I owe her that… and an apology…"

"So I can ask her to come to the house?"

"Yes Mary…"

"Okay..."

"You feel better now?"

"Yes..."

"Good... now let's finish eating – I made you a promise – and I intend to keep it..." he said and then he pulled me into a kiss...

"Mmmm... sounds good..." I said as we finished eating. I gulped down my orange juice, got up from the table, went to the bathroom, and turned on the shower. Wayne gulped down his orange juice, got up from the table, and went into the bathroom. I was in the shower already and when Wayne pulled back the curtain he was pleasantly surprised...

"Wow..." he said when he saw that I was on the bench doing a hand stand against the wall... "Hold that pose – I need to get a picture of this..." Wayne said as he ran to get his phone, took a picture, and put his phone down...

"Is your phone waterproof?"

"Yea..."

"Bring it in here..."

"Okay..." Wayne said as he walked into the shower and came over to me... "What now?"

"Put your dick in my mouth, pull me up so I can lock my legs around your neck, and hold me up..."

# Chapter 8

"Okay..." Wayne said as he positioned the phone to record what was about to go down. Once the phone was set to record, Wayne walked over to me, put his dick in my mouth, and lifted me up so I could lock my legs around his neck. Once I did that, Wayne was able to hold me in position so I could suck his dick while he had full access to my pussy. Wayne held me over the bench and we both went to work as the water beat down on us... "Mmmph... Mmmph... Mmmph... Mmmph..."

"Mmmm... Mmmm... Mmmm... Mmmm..." I took Wayne's dick in my mouth all the way down to his balls and it was angled perfectly to hit the back of my throat so I could deep throat him...

"Ummph... Ummph... Ummph... Ummph..." My pussy was wet and open and Wayne took full advantage, sticking his tongue deep inside...

"Hmmph! Hmmph! Hmmph! Hmmph!" I started swirling my tongue around Wayne's dick and started sucking him harder...

"Ummph! Ummph! Ummph! Ummph!" Wayne returned the fervor on my pussy as he alternated between swirling his tongue around my clit and sucking it...

"Hmmph! Hmmph! Hmmph! Hmmph!" Neither one of us could hold back as I took his dick all the way in my mouth and down the back of my throat and our legs shook...

"Ummph! Ummph! Ummph! Ummph Uuuummmmppppphhhhh!"

"Hmmph! Hmmph! Hmmph! Hmmph Hhhhmmmmmppppphhhhh!!" Wayne continued licking, slurping, and sucking until his dick went limp in my mouth and I spoke... "Wayne... put me down... I'm getting dizzy..." Wayne unclasped my legs from around his neck and gently laid me down on the bench and then he lifted me up... "Woa... I'm a little light headed..."

"Put your arms around my neck..."

"Okay..." I said as I wrapped my arms around Wayne's neck and he picked me up... "Where are we going?" I laughed...

"To bed..." Wayne answered as he carried me to the bed and sat me down. "Lay down..." Wayne commanded. I laid down on the bed... "Spread your legs..." I smiled and spread my legs. Wayne got on top of me, eased his dick inside me, pushed himself up on his hands, and started thrusting... "This is what happens when you suck my dick like you just did..." he growled...

"Ohhhh... Wayne... Yes..." I moaned as I spread my legs wider. Wayne grabbed my legs, lifted them up, and got on his knees... "Oh God!

Wayne! Yes!" I moaned as Wayne slammed his dick into me...

"You like this?"

"Yes! Oh God!"

"Uggh! Uggh! Uggh! Uggh!" Wayne put my legs up on his shoulders, stayed on his knees, and held me up by my ass as he continued fucking me...

"Oh God Wayne – You're so fuckin' deep!"

"You like it Mommy?"

"Yes Daddy yes! Fuck me! I'm cumming! I'm cumming! Aaaaggghhhh!"

"Uggh! Uggh! Uggh! Uggh! Uuuugggghhhh!" Wayne let my legs down and then he collapsed on top of me...

"I sure hope our shower has a bench..." I breathed...

"Why?"

"So I can suck your dick upside-down, get dizzy, and then you can fuck me right-side up!" I laughed...

"I can make sure we have a bench put in the shower..." Wayne said as he kissed me...

"I love you..." I breathed...

"I love you too..."

"How much time do we have left before checkout?"

"It's just about 10 a.m."

"Oh good – we can stay in bed until 11 – then get in the shower..."

"You ready for more?" Wayne asked...

"Hell yea!" I breathed as Wayne eased himself back inside me and put his tongue in my mouth...

"Mmmph...      Mmmph...      Mmmph... Mmmph..."

"Mmmm... Mmmm... Mmmm... Mmmm..."

# Chapter 9

"Hi Mommy..."

"Hi Starr – can you stop by after work?"

"I don't know..."

"Please? It's important..."

"Okay Mommy – I'll stop by..."

"Okay – I'll see you later..."

"She's coming?" Wayne asked...

"Yea – she's coming..."

"I guess I better get ready..." Wayne said as he went to get dressed...


"Hi Starr..."

"Hi Chandler..."

"What's wrong?"

"Mommy wants me to stop by after work..."

"You don't wanna go?"

"Not really..."

"So tell her that..."

"She said it was important..."

"I can meet you there if you want..."

"Yes... I want..."

"Okay – I'll pick you up at the train station and we'll go straight there..."

"Thank you Chandler – I love you..."

"I love you too..." Chandler said as he hung up...

"Is everything okay Starr?" Amy asked...

"Yea..."

"Are you sure?"

"Yea..."

"No it's not – what's wrong?"

"My mother wants me to come over after work..."

"Aww... that's nice..."

"I just want to go home..."

"So go home..."

"I don't want to upset my mother..."

"Starr?"

"Yes Amy?"

"You have to put yourself first..."

"I know... but she said it was important..."

"What do you want to do Starr?"

"Chandler's picking me up at the train station so I don't have to go by myself..."

"You don't have to go at all Starr..."

"I know..." she sighed.  Starr dreaded getting on the train.  Fortunately it was a local so she had time to ride and think.  When she got off the train she ran down the steps to get to Chandler...  "Hey..." she said as she jumped in the car...

"What'd you do – run down the stairs?"

"Yea..."

"Come here Starr..."

"Okay..." she said as she moved closer to Chandler and he kissed her

"Mmmm... that's nice..."

"I can be nicer..."

"I know..."

"Let's go to your mother's house..."

"Okay..." she sighed as she put on her seat belt and Chandler drove off. When they got to my house she hesitated to get out the car after Chandler opened the door for her...

"Starr... c'mon..."

"Okay..." she sighed as she got out.

"I gotchu – Okay?" Chandler said as he pulled her into a hug...

"I know..." she said as they walked up to my door and knocked...

"Who is it?"

"It's me Mommy..."

"Why didn't you use your key – oh – hi Chandler..." I said as she opened the door and saw Wayne sitting in the living room...

"What's he doing here Mommy?"

"Come sit down Starr..." I said without answering her question...

"I'm Wayne..." Wayne said as he reached out to shake Chandler's hand...

"I'm Chandler – Starr's husband..."

"I'm her step-father..."

"No you're not!" Starr snapped...

"Starr..." Wayne started to say...

"You lost the right to call me your daughter when you abandoned me..."

"You're right... I'm sorry..."

"Wow... thanks..."

"For what?"

"For acknowledging my feelings…"

"I know it's not an excuse – but I was devastated when I found out you weren't my biological daughter…"

"You were the only father I ever knew – why did that have to change?"

"You don't understand…"

"I don't understand…" Chandler interrupted…

"Chandler – no disrespect…"

"Let me stop you right there – you raised Starr for 18 years – you loved her right?"

"Yes…"

"So – you found out Bazil was her biological father – so you don't love her anymore?"

"It wasn't as simple as that…"

"You abandoned her when she needed you the most – her mother was in prison – you knew she wasn't in contact with her father – but that didn't matter – what mattered was how you felt about Bazil…"

"You're right…" Wayne said and then he turned to Starr… "Starr – I'm sorry – I never should have abandoned you – I know I can't make it up to you – or your mother – but I'd like to try…"

"I'm not sure how I feel about that…"

"I understand…"

"Starr?" my mother asked…

"Yes Mommy?"

"We have something we need to tell you…" I said as I took Wayne's hand…

"Your mother and I got married..." Wayne said...

"What?" Starr asked in shock...

"We were married yesterday..." I said...

"Wow... congratulations..." Starr laughed...

"Starr... don't be that way..." my mother sighed...

"I'm in shock Mommy – I didn't even know you and Wayne were seeing each other again..."

"We weren't..."

"I don't understand..."

"Wayne came to see me on Monday... we talked... he proposed... I said yes..."

"Do you even love Wayne Mommy?"

"Yes Starr..."

"How convenient..."

"Starr!"

"Wayne?"

"Yes Starr?"

"You love my mother?"

"I've always loved your mother Starr... I loved you both..."

"You know she loved my father – right?"

"Yes..."

"That doesn't bother you?"

"To be honest... it hurt me..."

"But you still wanted to marry my mother?"

"Your mother doesn't want your father anymore... she wants me..."

"So... why is this the first time I'm seeing you?"

"I didn't think you'd forgive me for abandoning you..."

"What about my mother?"

"I didn't think she wanted me – especially when I saw her with Jermoll..."

"Hol' up..." Chandler interrupted... "You've been stalking them?"

"I've been around... I've been watching Mary..."

"I should lock your ass up – you know I can lock your ass up for stalking them – right?"

"Yes..." Wayne sighed...

"Give me one good reason why I shouldn't take your ass outta here in handcuffs!" Chandler snapped...

"I came back for Mary..."

"You came back? Where the hell you been?"

"I stayed away because I didn't think they'd want me back in their lives..."

"I'm still not sure I want you back in my life..." Starr said...

"I understand..."

"Why now?" Chandler asked...

"I've been miserable without Mary..." Wayne said as he kissed my hand...

"And I've been miserable without you..." I said as I kissed Wayne...

"When Mary accepted my proposal I couldn't let her get away from me again..."

"Starr – I'm happy – please be happy for me..." I said...

"Okay Mommy – if you say so – but I do have a question..."

"Okay..."

"Now that you're married... is Wayne staying here?"

"No Starr... Wayne answered..."

"Where will you be staying?"

"Starr... we're moving to Ontario..." I answered...

"Ontario? Canada?"

"Yes..."

"When?"

"We're leaving Friday morning..."

"So – you got married yesterday – and you're leaving for Canada on Friday?"

"Yes Starr..."

"What about your grandchild?"

"I don't need to live here to be in my grandchild's life..."

"I'm confused – at the restaurant..."

"At the restaurant I was angry... and selfish..." I sighed. Chandler and Starr looked at each other in disbelief...

"Starr – I just want to love your mother and make her happy..." Wayne said...

"Okay... I guess..."

"What does that mean?"

"You abandoned me when I was 18 – I'm 22 – now you come back – you marry my mother – as if the last 4 years didn't happen – that's what it means..."

"Point taken..."

"Congratulations – if you're truly happy – I'm happy..." Chandler said...

"Do you have somewhere to stay? In Ontario?" Starr asked...

"Yes – Wayne bought a mobile home for us..."

"Will you be here for my baby shower?"

"I don't know Starr... you, Chandler, me, Wayne, your father, Beautiee..."

"So you're not coming back? Ever?"

"I don't know if I can be in the same room with your father Starr..." Wayne said...

"You've got some fucking nerve!" Starr snapped...

"Starr – I didn't mean it like that..."

"How did you mean it then?"

"To be honest... I don't know if your father can look at me without wanting to kill me..."

"What's that got to do with my mother?"

"Nothing..."

"Exactly – so why can't you come back to see your grandchild Mommy?"

"I didn't say that – I just said I might not be here for the baby shower..."

"I've heard enough – c'mon Chandler – let's go – goodbye mother..." Starr said as she walked out the door...

"Goodbye Wayne... goodbye Mary... good luck..." Chandler said as he got up and walked out...

"You still want me?" Wayne asked as he pulled me into a kiss...

"Yes Wayne..."

"Starr will calm down..."

"We can come back... right?"

"Mary?"

"Yes Wayne?"

"I'm not kidnapping you..."

"She's hurt..."

"Mary?"

"Yes Wayne?"

"Who deserves to be happy?"

"We do..."

"Who deserves to be happy?" he asked again as he kissed me deeply...

"Mmmm..... we do..."

"I just want us to start over... and be happy... we can't do that if we stay here..."

"I know..."

"Once we're settled... if you want to come visit... we'll come visit..."

"Okay..."

# Chapter 10

"Starr?"

"Yes Chandler?"

"You okay?"

"Yea..."

"You sure?"

"Yea..."

"How you feel about your mother getting married? Really?"

"Well... I'm kinda glad... but I also think she may be full of shit..."

"Really?"

"Yea..."

"Why?"

"Since she got out of jail – she never once mentioned Wayne – now she's so in love with him?"

"Starr – what are you saying?"

"I think Wayne loves her – but she still loves my dad..."

"Starr?"

"Yes Chandler?"

"So what?"

"Excuse me?"

"So what? Why does it matter to you?"

"I just want her to be honest... with herself..."

"What if she honestly needs Wayne to help her get over your father? If he's okay with it – I'm okay with it..."

"Really?"

"Starr – you keep telling your mother she's miserable – she's trying to be happy – let her be happy – okay?"

"You're right... I don't know how I feel about Wayne though..."

"I don't care about Wayne one way or the other – I'm just glad he married your mother..."

"You are?"

"Hell yea – it could've been anybody – as long as she's happy she won't make us miserable..."

"I guess..."

"Starr?"

"Yes Chandler?"

"What is it?"

"I remember how happy she was when she told me Jermoll proposed..."

"Jermoll proposed? To your mother?"

"Yes..."

"So... she was gonna marry Jermoll?"

"Yea..."

"Okay..."

"So now she loves Wayne..."

"Starr – they were together for 18 years – maybe they have unfinished business..."

"I never thought of it like that..."

"I think..." Chandler said as he pulled Starr into a kiss... "We should stop worrying about your mother... and Wayne..." he said as he kissed her neck... "And start thinking about how much nicer I can be..."

"Oooohhh... I love it when you're nice..."

"Come here..." Chandler said as he stopped kissing her and pulled her into the other room...

"Oh Chandler!" she exclaimed...

"I hope you like it..."

"I love it!" she squealed as she jumped into Chandler's arms...

"I love you Mrs. Corbett..." he breathed as he kissed her...

"I love you too... Mr. Corbett..." she moaned...

"I want to make love to you... right here..."

"In the baby's room?"

"Yes..."

"On the floor?"

"There's carpet..." Chandler whispered as he undressed her...

"Okay..." Starr watched Chandler get undressed and then he got down on his knees...

"Come here..." Chandler said as he took her hand and she got down on her knees in front of him. Chandler pulled her close, moved his hands up her back, held her against him, and kissed her hard...

"Chandler..." Chandler eased her down on the floor, laid on top of her, and spread her legs... "Oh... Chandler..." she moaned as Chandler spread her lips and sucked her clit...

"Mmmm...." Chandler moaned as he started licking up and down...

"Ohhh... Chandler..." Chandler held her legs apart, took her clit in his mouth, and started sucking hard... "Chandler... Huh... Chandler... Chandler..." Chandler put two fingers in her pussy and started finger-fucking her... "Chandler! Chandler! Chandler!" she screamed as she lifted her body of off the floor, her legs shook, and she grabbed his head... "I'm cumming! I'm cumming! I'm cumming!" Chandler continued finger-fucking her and sucking her clit even after her orgasm subsided as she moved around on the floor...

"You're still horny..." Chandler breathed as he moved up her body, layed on top of her, put his arms under her back, eased himself inside her, and started fucking her...

"Ohh... Ohh... Ohh... Ohh..." she moaned...

"Uggh... Uggh... Uggh... Uggh..." Starr pulled Chandler's face to her and kissed him hard. Chandler put his tongue in her mouth and she sucked on it. Chandler took her tongue in his mouth and sucked on it and they took turns sucking each other's tongues as Chandler continued fucking her...

"Huuhh... Huuhh... Huuhh... Huuhh..."

"Mmmph... Mmmph... Mmmph... Mmmph..." Starr moved her hands down to Chandler's ass, squeezed it, spread her legs wider, and pushed him in deeper...

"Haahh... Haahh... Haahh... Haahh..."

"Damn... you're so fuckin' wet... Ugghh..."

"Chandler... Oh God... Chandler..." Chandler flipped her over and she was now on top of him. Chandler sat up, braced himself against the dresser, grabbed her ass, and pushed her down on his dick as she bent her legs...

"Remember the first time you wanted to try this on me?"

"Yes Chandler..." she moaned...

"Is it good?"

"Yes Chandler... Ohhh..."

"Come for me..."

"Huhh... Huhh... Huhh... Huhh..."

"That's it... come for me Starr..." Starr wrapped her arms around Chandler's neck, threw her head back, and rode Chandler's dick harder as he grabbed her ass...

"Aaagh... Aaagh... Aaagh... Aaagh... Aaagh... Aaaaaggggghhhhh!" Starr continued riding Chandler's dick as he quickened his pace...

"Uggh! Uggh! Uggh! Uggh! Uuuggghhh!"

"Chandler..." Starr whispered. Chandler flipped her onto her back and started fucking her again...

"Chandler..." Chandler spread her legs, put them up on his shoulders, and came back down on top of her with her legs spread wide... "Chandler... Ooohhh... Ooohhh... Oooohhh..." Chandler started kissing her as he kept her legs open and she was so turned on...

"Huhh... Huhh... Huhh... Huhh..." she moaned into Chandler's mouth...

"Huhh... Huhh... Huhh... Huhh..." he moaned into her mouth...

"Come Chandler..." she breathed. Chandler kept her legs spread wide and fucked her harder...

"Starr... Fuck... I'm cumming..."

"I'm cumming with you Chandler..."

"Starr... Uuugh... Uuugh... Uuugh... Uuugggghhhh!"

"Chandler... Aaahhh... Aaahhh... Aaaaggghhhh!" Chandler put her legs down but stayed inside her as they kissed each other...

"Starr... what the fuck..."

"Maybe we waited too long..."

"It's only been a couple of days..."

"I missed you Chandler..."

"I missed you too..."

"I won't wait this long again Chandler... I need it..."

"I need it too..."

"I can't believe we fucked on the floor of our child's room..." she laughed...

"Shit – I can!" Chandler laughed...

"We only have a few rooms left..." she laughed...

"You'll be pregnant for a few months – we'll get it done..."

"Okay – we need to do it in the kitchen..."

"We started in the kitchen..." Chandler laughed...

"We need to finish in the kitchen..." she laughed...

"Shit – I can put you on the island and have dessert!"

"Ooohhh... Okay!"

"I can take you in the guest room..."

"And you can take me in the shower..."

"We've already done that..."

"I mean take me in the guest shower..."

"Okay..."

"Oh my God!" she said and then she bust out laughing...

"What's so funny?"

"I just imagined my mother catching us in the kitchen..." she laughed...

"I'ma take you in there and fuck you on purpose..." Chandler laughed...

"I love you Chandler..."

"I love you too..." Chandler said as he kissed her... "Let's go to bed..."

"Okay..." Starr sighed as Chandler helped her up off the floor...

"Can you take Friday off?"

"Sure – if you want – why?"

"I want to meet my mother at the train and see her off."

# Chapter 11

"Good morning Amy..." Starr said as she walked in...

"Good morning Starr – did you go to your mother's house last night?"

"Yea..."

"You okay?"

"Yea..."

"So... what was so important?"

"Well..."

"Never mind – it's none of my business..."

"She got married..."

"Really? That's great! Wait a minute – that's great... right?"

"Yea..."

"You sure?"

"I'm not – but she is..."

"Do you know her husband?"

"Yea... he's okay..."

"Does he love your mother?"

"Definitely..."

"Aww... well tell her I said congratulations..."

"I won't be in Friday..."

"Everything alright?"

"My mother's leaving..."

"Oh wow – they're going on their honeymoon?"

"My mother's moving to Ontario..."

"On Friday?"

"Yea..."

"Oh wow..."

"That's what I said..."

"Oh so you wanna see her off..."

"Yea..."

"What time is she leaving?"

"7 a.m...."

"Does she know you're coming?"

"No..."

"Aww... you're going to surprise her..."

"Yea... she might not be here for my baby shower..."

"Honey – she'll be here for his birth..."

"A boy?"

"Probably – I'm usually right about these things..." Starr went over to Amy and hugged her tight... "Aww... you want a boy..."

"I want both..."

"A boy and a girl?"

"I don't care..." she sighed...

"Well I'm glad you're so happy..."

"We are..."

"I'm stepping out for coffee – you want some?"

"Sure – thanks..." she said as she picked up her cell phone...

"Hi Starr..."

"Hi Daddy..."

"Everything okay?"

"I have some news..."

"You're having twins?"

"I don't know yet..." she laughed...

"Okay... tell me..."

"Mommy got married on Monday..."

"Did she?"

"Yea..."

"I didn't know your mother was dating – tell her I said congratulations..."

"She married Wayne Daddy..."

"He's back?"

"Yea..."

"Where's he been?"

"I don't know... but he told Chandler he's been watching Mommy..."

"He was?"

"He said he didn't let Mommy know he was here right away because he wasn't sure if we wanted him back in our lives..."

"Hmmm... interesting..."

"He told Chandler he was my step-father – I said no you're not – you lost the right to call me your daughter when you abandoned me..."

"What'd he say?"

"He said I had a right to feel the way I feel..."

"Okay..."

"He really loves Mommy..."

"Does he?"

"Yea... I just hope Mommy loves him too..."

"They were together a long time – I'm sure she loves him..."

"I just want Mommy to be happy..."

"She is Starr..."

"You think so?"

"Yes..."

"I asked Mommy if Wayne was going to live with her – she said they're moving to Ontario..."

"Ontario?"

"Yea – and they're leaving Friday morning..."

"Is that right?"

"Yea – Mommy said Wayne bought them a mobile home..."

"Yea – with my money..." Bazil mumbled...

"What Daddy?"

"Nothing – Starr – I'm getting another call – I have to call you back..." Bazil said as he hung up...

"Who was that?" Beautiee asked as she fed Jay...

"That was Starr..."

"How's she doing?"

"She said Mary got married..."

"Really?"

"Yea..."

"Thank God – now she can get some dick!" Beautiee laughed...

"Starr said they're leaving for Ontario on Friday..."

"Canada? Wow..."

"Starr said Wayne bought them a mobile home..."

"Oh... that's nice – at least they won't be homeless..."

"No... they won't..." Bazil said as he left the room...

"Bazil – where are you?"

"I'm downstairs – I'll be up in a minute..." he said and then he made a call...

"Hello Mr. Osgood – how are you?"

"Angry..."

"What do you need me to do?"

"I need you to run a facebook profile and a title search..."

"What's the name?"

"Wayne Robinson..."

"Can you give me any pertinent information?"

"He was married to Mary Smith on Monday, June 24th, Bridgeport, CT..."

"That's easy to obtain – that's public information..."

"He bought a mobile home in Ontario..."

"Canada?"

"Yes..."

"Hmmm – I'll get on this asap..."

"Thank you Conrad."

# Chapter 12

"Hello..."

"He knows..."

"You told him?"

"Starr told him..."

"Shit!"

"This could be a good thing..."

"I hope so..."

"You'll be leaving in a few days..."

"She wants to come back..."

"Fuck!"

"She wants to see her grandchild..."

"I'd wanna see my grandchild too..."

"I'm happy Starr's happy but I wish they'd come to Canada so we don't have to come back here..."

"Maybe they will..."

"I doubt it..."

"I'll suggest it to Starr – I'll tell her how beautiful Canada is..."

"Thank you – I appreciate that..."

"It's the least I can do..."

"I need to see Bazil..."

"I don't know if that's a good idea..."

"I don't have a choice..."

"Why?"

"Starr wants us to come back for her baby shower..."

"Oh..."

"I told her I didn't think I could be in the same room with her father without him wanting to kill me..."

"I don't think you should see Bazil..."

"What about the baby shower?"

"It's usually women at these things – but since we probably won't be there – you should be okay..."

"Why won't you be there?"

"You saw what happened at the restaurant..."

"So Bazil won't be there..."

"No..."


"I didn't expect you to call me back this fast..."

"I have something..."

"What is it?"

"Check your email..."

"Okay – thanks..." Bazil said as he hung up, turned on his computer, and opened the email from Conrad. Bazil's heart sank as he read the attachments:


"Hi Wayne, I'm Bazil's wife. You came across my timeline as someone I may know so I wanted to reach out to you. I'm reaching out to you because I'm concerned about Mary. She's miserable and she's making our lives miserable.

I love Starr and I want to have a good relationship with her but Mary is getting in the way. To be honest, I think she still has feelings for my husband and she can't let go of him. She's been living downtown in Bridgeport since she got out of prison. If you're the least bit curious about her I'll give you her address."

"Do I look like an April fool? The fuck I look like talkin' to you? So... you expect me to believe you're just going to give me Mary's address? Why would I trust you?" How the fuck do I know you're not setting me up? Tell Bazil I said hi – nice try... Haa haa haa!"

"I don't blame you for being suspicious. Bazil has nothing to do with why I reached out to you – well – he does in a way – she's making his life miserable too – but Bazil didn't ask me to contact you – Bazil doesn't know anything about this. I reached out to you because I thought since you were in a relationship with her, maybe you still having feelings for her and you can make her happy."

"Make her happy? What makes you think she isn't happy the way she is?" She's been out of prison and hasn't even thought about me! She doesn't want anything to do with me!"

"Maybe she thinks you don't want anything to do with her. Maybe the reason she's so miserable is because she hasn't found love since you parted ways."

"You must really think I'm stupid!"

"Aren't you the least bit curious? You were together for 18 years – you raised Starr – you must still have some feelings?"

"I have feelings alright – and they're not all good..."

"So you do have some good feelings?"

"I still love her..."

"I thought so..."

"What's in this for you?"

"If there's a chance you can make Mary happy... that's all I need."

"Okay.... Give me her address..."

"Call me – 203-578-2798."

Bazil closed out the conversation and opened the title search:

## Property Information

Owner Name: Wayne Robinson
County: Ontario County
Address:
201 East Arrow Highway,
Toronto Ontario M1E4Y1
Report Created on: 6/24/19
Legal Description: Mfd/Mobile Home
Deed Information: Warranty Deed
Title Vested in:
Wayne Robinson, Single Male
Title Received From:
Tracy Wilson, Married Female
Dated: 6/15/19  Recorded: 6/24 19
Book & Page: 12345/2019
1st Mortgage: 21,000
Dated: 6/15/17  Recorded: 6/15/07
ORB 12345/2017
Lender: Bank of New York
Borrower: Tracy Wilson
2nd Mortgage: Cash
Dated: 6/15/19  Recorded" 6/24/19
ORB 67890/201
Lender: N/A
Borrower: N/A

## Leins, Judgement & Comments: None

## Tax Information

Tax ID: 12345-67-89-0123
Tax Year: 2019
Date Paid: 6/15/19  Amount: $10,000
Assessed Value: $45,000

"Hmmm... you just closed on this recently... good..." Bazil said as he called Conrad...

"Hello..."

"They're leaving on Friday morning..."

"When do you need the project completed?"

"They'll be there on Saturday morning..." Bazil answered as he hung up. Bazil closed out his email, turned off the computer, and went into the kitchen to make coffee... "Beautiee – you comin' downstairs?" he called out...

"I'll be right down Bazil ..." she answered... "I gotto go..." Beautiee said as she hung up... "C'mon Jay – Daddy wants us..." she said as she got up, put on her slippers, picked up Jay, and went downstairs to the kitchen... "Hey..." Beautiee said as she went over to Bazil and went to kiss him but he turned his head away... "No Kiss?"

"Sit down Beautiee..."

"Kiss me Bazil..." Bazil gave Beautiee a quick kiss and went back to making coffee... "Okay – that's it..." Beautiee said as she went to get the swing. Bazil watched as Beautiee left and then came back with the swing, dragging it into the kitchen with one hand and holding Jay under her arm...

"Beautiee – let me help you..."

"I got it!" Beautiee snapped as she put Jay in the swing and sat down at the table. Bazil sat down at the table and gave Beautiee a cup of coffee... "What's wrong? You barely kissed me!"

"I'm going to ask you a question..." Bazil said and then he took a sip of coffee... "When I told you Mary was married – you already knew – didn't you?"

"Yes..." Beautiee answered as she drank her coffee...

"How long have you been communicating with Wayne?"

"A few weeks..."

"Why didn't you tell me?"

"I didn't want to..."

"That hurts me... and it also makes me angry..."

"I've been hurt... and I've been angry... so I know exactly how you feel..."

"No Beautiee... you don't..."

"Really?"

"I saw the chat between you... and Wayne..."

"Oh..."

"That's all you have to say?"

"From the day I found out I was pregnant – the same day I found out you lied to me about your daughter..."

"I never lied to you..."

"Oh – that's right – you just forgot to mention a daughter you had with the woman you cheated on your wife with – who I was also in prison with – who you also pushed me away for – you know what – fuck her – and fuck you too – I should'a just killed the Bitch like I started to‐ but no – after everything that Bitch did to you – to me – to our son – oh shit – I know why you're really mad – she can't let go of you – and you can't let go of her!" Beautiee snapped as she got up from the table...

"Beautiee... I'm sorry..." Bazil whispered as he grabbed her hand...

"No – you're not sorry – I am!" Beautiee snapped as she snatched her hand away from Bazil and stormed out the kitchen...

"Daddy will be right back..." Bazil sighed as he got up and went after Beautiee. Bazil caught her on the stairs, pulled her into his arms, and carried her back downstairs... "Now..." he said as he turned her around to face him... "You're going to come back into the kitchen... I'm going to make us breakfast... and we're going to talk..." he said and then he kissed her passionately...

"Okay..." Beautiee breathed. Bazil went back into the kitchen and Beautiee followed. He went into the refrigerator and took out eggs, cheese, potatoes, bacon, and biscuits. Beautiee sat at the table watching Bazil make breakfast as she played with Jay. When the food was done, Bazil put the plates on the table and Jay started fussing...

"What's wrong Jay?" Bazil asked...

"Here Jay..." Beautiee said as she took the fork, smashed up some potatoes, and put it in Jay's mouth...

"Are you sure that's okay?"

"My grandfather used to do this with all his grandchildren..." Beautiee said as she mashed up some more potatoes and put them in his mouth...

"Okay... I'm sorry..."

"For what?"

"For being angry at you because you didn't tell me..."

"Okay..."

"I thought you wanted Wayne to kill Mary..."

"To be honest... I did..."

"Beautiee..."

"I know he loves her – and I'm glad they worked things out – but after she said what she said at the restaurant – I wanted her to die..."

"I'm sorry..."

"I had to get her out of our lives – one way or another..."

"I was going to talk to her..."

"I told you – I'm all talked out – that Bitch needed to be taken down – and now..." Beautiee sighed as she smiled... "She has been..."

"We're you ever going to tell me?"

"I don't know – I was just so happy – it seems like we can't ever be happy without someone trying to ruin it..."

"I'm sorry..."

"I swear – if you tell me you're sorry one more fuckin' time..."

"I'm sorry..." Bazil said as he smiled mischievously...

"Jay – I'ma need to turn you around for a minute..." Beautiee said as she turned the swing around and turned it on so Jay could swing on his own. Beautiee went over to Bazil, opened her robe, straddled Bazil, sat on his dick, and put her tongue in his mouth. Bazil moved his hands up Beautiee's back, held her tight, and began kissing her fiercely as she rode his dick...

"Mmmph... Mmmph... Mmmph... Mmmph..."

"Mmmm... Mmmm... Mmmm... Mmmm...." Bazil stopped kissing Beautiee, took her left breast in his mouth, and sucked as she continued ridding his dick...

"Mmmph... Mmmph... Mmmph... Mmmph..."

"Haah... Haah... Haah... Haah...."

"That's it... ride my dick..." Bazil growled as he grabbed her ass and pushed her down on his dick...

"Bazil... Fuck... Haah... Haah..."

"Uggh... Uggh... Uggh... Uggh..."

"Bazil... I'm cumming... I'm cumming... I'm cumming..."

"Cum for me..."

"Aaah... Aaah... Aaah... Aaah... Aaaaagh!"

"Uggh! Uggh! Uggh! Uggh! Ugggghhhh!" Beautiee took Bazil's face in her hands, put her tongue in his mouth, and kissed him hard...

"Mmmm... you're still horny..." he said as they continued kissing...

"Mmmm hmmm..."

"You want more..."

"Mmmm hmmm..."

"Say please..."

"Please... My Thirst Quencher... may I... have... some... more?"

"Let's go upstairs... and I'll give you more..."

"Okay..." Beautiee breathed. Beautiee stood up and when she went to turn the swing around she saw that Jay had fallen asleep so she picked Jay up out the swing and they went upstairs.

# Chapter 13

"Starr..." Chandler whispered as he kissed her neck...

"Huh?" she answered sleepily...

"We need to get ready..."

"I'm not going to work today..."

"Starr..."

"Yes... Chandler..."

"We need to get ready..." he whispered as he kissed her...

"Mmmm... okay... I'm ready..." she said as she rolled on her back...

"Starr..."

"Yes... Chandler..."

"Your mother's leaving today..."

"Okay..." Starr said as she wrapped her arms around Chandler and kissed him...

"Starr..."

"Yes... Chandler..." she said between kisses...

"We can't do this..."

"Please?"

"Starr... I need to stay awake..."

"What time is it?"

"It's 5 a.m...."

"Okay..." she answered as she got up...

"You're okay – right?"

"Yea... I'm just sleepy..."

"We need to be at Penn Station by 7 a.m. – the train leaves at 7:15..."

"Okay..." she said as she went to the bathroom...

"Good morning..." Chandler said as he came up behind her and kissed her on her neck...

"Good morning – what time are we leaving?"

"Soon as we throw some water on our face... and get dressed..."

"Okay – thank God we have two sinks..." Starr said as she went to one sink and Chandler went to the other...

"We can stop for coffee and then we'll be on our way..."

"Okay..." Starr said as she hurried into the bedroom...

"Starr... wait..."

"Yes Chandler?" Chandler walked over to Starr, pulled her to him from behind, held her, and put his hands on her stomach...

"I love you..." he breathed in her ear...

"I love you too..."

"Okay... let's get dressed... before we get in trouble..."

"Okay..." she laughed as she got dressed. After they got dressed, they headed out the door and ran into Theresa and Charles...

"Good morning!" Charles said...

"Good morning..." Chandler said...

"Mornin' y'all – I'm sleepy..." Theresa said...

"Morning... so am I..." Starr yawned as they all got in the elevator...

"Where y'all headed?" Chandler asked...

"I'on know... Charles wants to go out to eat..." Theresa yawned...

"Me too..." Starr yawned...

"Oh yea? Where?" Charles asked...

"My mother's..." Starr answered...

"Okay – have a nice day – see y'all later..." Charles said as they headed out...

"Nice save..." Chandler laughed...

"Thanks – I didn't wanna explain..."

"I know – c'mon – it's just about 5:30 – we should get there by 10 minutes to 7 – that'll give us enough time to see them off..."

"Okay..." Starr sighed. Chandler opened the door, Starr got in, and then he got in...

"Starr..." Chandler said as he took Starr's hand...

"Yes Chandler?"

"Look at me..."

"Yes Chandler?"

"We can go visit them in Canada..."

"We can?"

"Of course... we can meet them in Niagara Falls..."

"I've always wanted to go to Niagara Falls..." she sighed...

"Let's get going..." Chandler said as he started the car and they headed over to Dunkin Donuts. Chandler pulled in front of Dunkin

Donuts and parked the car... "I'll be right back..."

"Okay..." she said as Chandler went inside... and ran right into Charles..."

"Hey!" Charles exclaimed... "I didn't know you were tailing me..."

"Oh you got jokes..." Chandler laughed...

"I thought you were going to your mother's?"

"We are – she doesn't have any coffee..." Chandler said as he left before Charles could ask any more questions...

"Here..." Chandler laughed as he handed Starr coffee...

"What's so funny"

"Charles..."

"In there?"

"Yea – I told him your mother doesn't have any coffee..."

"Oh – that was quick thinking..." Starr laughed as they drove off. Fortunately traffic wasn't too bad on 95 South and they were able to make it to Penn Station a little before 7 a.m. Chandler was able to park right in front and no one would ever question a Sergeant... or so he thought...

"Good morning – Sergeant?"

"Yes Sir..."

"What brings you down to Penn Station so early?"

"Business..."

"Down here? At this hour?"

"Crime never sleeps..."

"You got that right – you need any assistance?"

"I got it – thanks…" Chandler said as he took Starr's hand and went to walk inside…

"Your daughter is beautiful…"

"She's my wife – but thanks…" Chandler said as they hurried inside and went to look at the board…

"Chandler – Gate 73 West…" Starr read…

"This way…" Chandler said as they ran towards Gate 73 west. When the got there Starr could see me but I didn't know she was there…

"I'm so excited!" I said as I grabbed Wayne by the arm…

"Me too…" Wayne said…

"I've always wanted to go to Niagara Falls…"

"And I've always wanted to take you…" Wayne said as he pulled me into his arms and kissed me…"

"Ahem!" Starr said as she interrupted us…

"Excuse me – le'me tell you something…" I said as I turned around and burst into tears when I saw Starr…

"Mommy!" she said as she threw her arms around me as I cried…

"Starr – I love you so much…"

"I love you too Mommy…"

"You're not mad at me?"

"For what?"

"For leaving?"

"Mommy – I just want you to be happy…"

"I am Starr..." I said as I took Wayne's hand...

"Good morning Starr – good morning Chandler..." Wayne said...

"Good morning Wayne – sorry..." Starr laughed as she hugged him and it made me smile...

"Good morning Mary – good morning Wayne..." Chandler said...

"Do you have a phone Mommy?"

"Do we Wayne?" I asked...

"Not yet..."

"Just call me on my cell – and send me pictures – I need to see every sonogram and I want pictures of your belly..."

"I will Mommy – as soon as I find a doctor that delivers babies..."

"Ask Dr. Julianne for one..."

"Okay – I will..."

"Call us when you get settled – we'll meet up in Niagara Falls..." Chandler said...

"I'd like that..." Wayne said...

"Train to Niagara Falls – Gate 73 West – now boarding..."

"Bye Mommy!" Starr said as she grabbed me, hugged me tight, and started crying...

"Starr – you're gonna make me cry – stop it..." I said as I hugged her back and teared up...

"Have a nice trip..." Chandler said as he shook Wayne's hand...

"Thank you Chandler..."

"Bye Wayne..." Starr said as she hugged Wayne...

"Bye Starr..."

"Good bye Mary..." Chandler said as he hugged me..."

"Good bye Chandler – take care of my baby girl..."

"Absolutely..." Chandler said...

"We'll give you a call when we get settled in – we'll be arriving a little after 8..."Wayne said as he took my hand and we walked through the gate...

"Starr..." Chandler whispered as he pulled her into a hug, held her, and she cried on his shoulder...

"I miss her already..."

"We'll go visit as soon as they get settled – I promise..."

"Okay..."

"Please don't cry..." Chandler said as he started tearing up...

"I can't help it..."

"I know... it's okay..." he said and then he lifted her face up by her chin and kissed her...

"I love you Sergeant Corbett..."

"Ooohhh... I like that..." he said and then he kissed her again...

"I love you Sergeant Corbett..."

"Just so you know... when you get back home... I'm gonna give you what you asked me for earlier..." he said as he kissed her again...

"Ooohhh... I love it when you're nice to me..." she said as she kissed him back...

"Hey Sergeant – you good?" the NYPD officer asked as he walked up on them kissing...

"I'm great – c'mon Starr..." Chandler said as he wrapped his arm around Starr and they walked out of Penn Station arm in arm.

# Chapter 14

"Hello Conrad..."

"Good afternoon Bazil..."

"How's everything?"

"Everything's right on schedule..."

"Glad to hear it..."

"They'll be arriving in Niagara Falls at 4:54 p.m. and they'll be leaving Niagara Falls at 6:10 p.m...."

"How Romantic..."

"They'll be arriving in Ontario at 8:06 p.m...."

"A perfect summer evening..."

"Yes... I'm sure they'll enjoy a cozy romantic evening by the fire..."

"Perfect beginning for newlyweds..."

"They had a nice send off earlier..."

"Did they?"

"Yes – your daughter and her husband were there..."

"I'm sure that made her mother very happy..."

"Yes it did..."

"I'm glad they've reconciled..."

"I'll keep you posted..."

"Thank you Conrad..."

"I'm so happy..." I sighed...

"I love you Mrs. Robinson..." Wayne said as he kissed me...

"Mmmm.... I love you too Mr. Robinson..." Wayne pulled me close to him, put his arm around me, and whispered in my ear...

"You ever do it on a train?"

"No!"

"You ever thought about it?"

"Yes..."

"Interesting..." Wayne whispered as he started kissing my neck...

"Wayne... we can't..."

"Tonight... when we cross over from the United States into Canada..." he whispered as he bit my earlobe... "I'm going to finger-fuck you..." he continued to whisper as he put his hand between my legs and started rubbing my crotch... "Right here..."

"Oh God – I'm getting wet just thinking about it..." I breathed as I put my hand between his legs and started rubbing his dick through his pants...

"Good morning – tickets please..." the conductor interrupted. Thank God we had the cover around us so she couldn't see what we were doing...

"Good morning – here you are..." Wayne said as he handed the tickets to the conductor...

"Hmmm... one way to Ontario – how was your vacation?"

"It was wonderful..." I sighed...

"So do you live in Ontario now?" the conductor asked as she tore off part of the tickets...

"Yes..." Wayne answered...

"Okay – I need to see your passports – you'll need to show them again when you arrive in Niagara Falls because you're actually getting off in Canada – you'll need to show them again when you re-board the train in Niagara Falls – and you'll need to show them again in Ontario..." she said as she gave Wayne back the tickets and the passports...

"Thank you..." Wayne said...

"Where's your food car?" I asked...

"The food car is two cars down – we're still serving breakfast in the dining room if you're hungry..."

"Thank you – c'mon Wayne – let's go..." I said as I got up...

"Yes Dear..." Wayne said as he got up...

"Aww... - I love that..." the conductor said as she went to another passenger. When we got to the dining room the tables were set with table cloths and silverware...

"Oh wow... this is nice..." I said as I sat down at one of the tables. Wayne sat down across from me, took my hands, leaned forward, and kissed me...

"Thank you..."

"For what?"

"For letting me love you the way I've always wanted to..."

"Wayne... you're gonna make me cry..."

"As long as they're happy tears..."

"Good morning..." the waiter said as he came over to the table... "May I start you off with coffee?"

"Yes please!" I said...

"And you sir?"

"Yes – thank you..." After he poured us coffee he gave each of us a menu...

"I'll give you a minute to look over the menu – when you're ready just wave at me..."

"Okay – thank you..." Wayne said as we looked at the menu...

"Ohhh... I want the pancakes... and the big breakfast..." I said...

"I guess you're hungry..." Wayne laughed...

"Hungry... and nervous..."

"Why?"

"I just am..."

"So you eat when you're nervous?"

"Yea..."

"I'm nervous too..."

"You? Why?"

"We haven't lived together in a long time..."

"And that makes you nervous?"

"A little..."

"I'm glad you told me..."

"Me too..."

"Are you ready to order?" the waiter asked as he came over to the table...

"Yes – we'll have pancakes – and we'll also have the big breakfast..." Wayne answered...

"How would you like your eggs?"

"Scrambled... for both of us..."

"Bacon or sausage?"

"Sausage..."

"Okay – I'll be right back..." the waiter said as he went to put our order in...

"I still can't believe we're married..." I said...

"We are..."

"I'm sorry..."

"For what?"

"I'm sorry I didn't look for you..."

"I'm sorry too... but we can spend the rest of our lives making it up to each other..."

"Yes... we can..."

"Here's your pancakes..." the waiter said as he put them down on the table... "and... here's your breakfast – can I get you more coffee?"

"No thank you..." Wayne answered...

"Very well – here's your check – pay whenever you're ready..." he said as he went over to another table...

"Oh my God – these pancakes are delicious!" I exclaimed...

"They are good..." Wayne agreed...

"You've eaten in the dining car before?" I asked...

"A few times..."

"Is the food always this good?"

"Yes..."

"Hmmm... I'ma have to go online and write a nice review..." I said. Wayne and I finished eating as we looked out the window enjoying the view.  When we were finished eating, we went back to our seats and I snuggled up under him.  I took out my cell phone and checked in on facebook, liked some posts, took some pictures, and posted them.  I caught Wayne smiling at me a few times as he would stop looking out the window to look at me... "Wayne?"

"Yes Mary?"

"I wanna take a selfie..."

"Okay..." Wayne said as he smiled and posed for the selfie...  "Take another one..." Wayne said as he took the phone from me.  I watched as the numbers counted down and just as it got to number one, he kissed me... and it was perfect...  "Post that one..."

"Okay..." I said as I posted it, and then I sent it to Starr...

"Aww... hi Mommy – I miss you..." she text me...

"I miss you too..." I text her back as I snuggled back up under Wayne and we both went to sleep...

"Ladies and Gentleman – we're getting ready to cross over from the United States into Canada – please have your passports ready..." the conductor announced...

"Wayne..." I said as I stretched... and he slipped his hands in my pants and started playing with my clit... "Wayne..."

"Shhh... spread your legs..." he whispered as he turned towards me, pulled my head down towards his shoulder, and pushed his fingers inside me... "Bite me if you need to..." he whispered in my ear as he fucked me with his hand...

"Wayne... uuuggg..." I breathed into his chest as I grabbed him...

"Yes... that's it... give me that juice..." he whispered in my ear as he continued fucking me with his hand...

"Uuuggg..." I gritted through my teeth as I bit his shirt and tore it...

"Yes Mary... imagine this is my dick... fuck my hand..." Wayne breathed in my ear. I came up out my seat, got on my knees, and bit his shoulder...

"Ugghhh..... Uggghhh..... Ugggghhh..." I gritted as he pushed his fingers in deeper...

"Yes Mary... Fuck my hand... just like that..." he growlwed in my ear... and I lost it...

'Ugh! Ugh! Ugh! Ugh! Uuuuggghhhh!" I gritted as I came all over his hand and my body shook...

"Oh yes... I know that was good..." he whispered in my ear and then he kissed my neck and fucked me a little more until I stopped shaking. Wayne pulled his hand out my pants, put two fingers in his mouth, licked them, and then put one finger in my mouth... "Taste it..." he whispered as I sucked his finger dry and then I sat back down in my seat. Wayne leaned over, pulled my fact to his, put his tongue in my mouth, and kissed me hard...

"Mmmm...        Mmmm...        Mmmm... Mmmm..."

"Mmmph...    Mmmph...    Mmmph... Mmmph..."

"Spread your legs..." I whispered as I took my sweater, covered his crotch, unzipped his pants, and took his dick in my hand...

"Mary..." Wayne whispered...

"Ssshhh..." I whispered as I got up on my knees and pulled his head down towards my breasts. Wayne unbuttoned my blouse, took my right breast out of my bra, and sucked hard as I stroked his dick... and it was turning me on...

"Mmmph...    Mmmph...    Mmmph... Mmmph..." I had to bite down on my blouse to keep from moaning...

"Mmmmf...    Mmmmf...    Mmmmf... Mmmmf..." Wayne took my left breast out and started flicking his tongue up, down, and around my nipple as his dick got harder and he fucked my hand...

"Huh... Huh... Huh... Huh..." I was so turned on feeling his hot breath on my breast I jerked his dick harder as he took my breast in his mouth...

"Mmmmf...    Mmmmf...    Mmmmf... Mmmmf..." If it wasn't for me biting down on my shirt muffling my sounds the whole car would have heard me as Wayne sucked harder and rose up out the seat to fuck my hand...

"Mmmph! Mmmph! Mmmph! Mmmph! Mmmph! Mmmmppphhhh!" I continued stroking Wayne as he shot in my hand, slid back down his seat, stopped sucking my breast, and picked up my hand...

"What are you doing?" I whispered...

"I'm curious..." he whispered as he licked my hand... "Hmmm... now I know why you swallow..." he whispered as he pulled my face to his and kissed me hard...

"Oh my God... I can't wait to get off this train..." I breathed...

"Why?" Wayne breathed as he kissed me again... "What do you want?"

"I want you to fuck me... outside..."

"I can do that..."

"Attention passengers – we'll be pulling into the station in five minutes – please have your bags and your passports ready..."

"Ready?" I asked...

"Hell yea..." Wayne breathed as we stood in the aisle. Wayne took my hand and kissed it as we waited for everyone in front of us to stop off the train and it was finally our turn...

"Bags here please..." the conductor said. Wayne put the bags to the side...

"Tickets please..." Wayne gave her the tickets...

"Welcome to Canada – please take your bags..." the conductor said as Wayne took the bags and then we stopped off the train...

"Welcome to Canada – passports please..." another conductor said...

"Thank you – here ya go..." Wayne said as he handed the conductor our passports...

"Hmmm..." the conductor said as he looked at our passports...

"Something wrong?" Wayne asked...

"Maam – may I see your license?"

"Sure..." I said as I took it out and handed it to him...

"Okay – you're good to go · thanks..." he said as he handed my license back to me and handed the passports back to Wayne...

"May I ask why you needed to see my wife's license?"

"Your wife just recently got her passport – we always double-check new passports – sorry if I made you uncomfortable..."

"Not at all... I was just curious..."

"How long have ya been married?"

"Four days..."

"Four days? You're newlyweds?"

"Yes..." Wayne sighed as he pulled me close to him and wrapped his arm around me...

"Aww... congratulations... enjoy your honeymoon – I've got to get home to my wife – good night..."

"Good night..." we said in unison as he walked away...

"Let's go put our bags inside..." Wayne said...

"Okay..." I said and then I followed him inside and we went to the window...

"How may I help you?"

"We'd like to put our bags back there... with you... if that's alright..." Wayne said...

"Sure – just make sure you're back here at 5:45 for boarding..."

"Thank you..." Wayne said and then he took me by the hand and pulled me out the door...

"Where are we going?" I laughed as he continued pulling me...

"Over there... by the falls..."

"Okay..." I laughed as we hurried over to the falls... "Wayne... it's beautiful..." I whispered as the sun started to go down and they turned on the lights in the falls...

"It's beautiful..." Wayne said as he took out his phone, pulled me close to him, and took a selfie...

"Send it to me so I can post it..."

"I will..." Wayne said as he kissed my neck... "Now... you said something..." he said as he kissed me again... "about fucking... outside..."

"Wayne... we can't..."

"See that tree over there?"

"Yes..."

"We can go behind that tree..."

"What if we get caught?"

"I'll lay you down... near the bushes..."

"Okay..." I said. Wayne took me by the hand, walked me over to the tree... and we stopped before he could get me to the bushes...

"Oh yes... fuck me..." we heard...

"Ugh... Ugh... Ugh..."

"Right there... yes... don't stop..."

"Ugh... Ugh... Ugh..."

"Oh God... I'm cumming... I'm cumming..."

"Ugh... ugh... ugh... ugh... Uuuuggghhhh!"

"Shit – what time is the train?" she breathed...

"5:45!" Wayne yelled as we jumped behind the tree so they couldn't see us...

"Oh my God! Get up!" she yelled as we watched them scrambling to pull up their pants and fix their clothes. When they ran off we both bust out laughing...

"Oh my God..." I laughed as I held my stomach...

"That made my night!" Wayne laughed...

"You scared the shit outta them!" I laughed...

"I know!" Wayne laughed...

"I'm sorry..."

"For what?"

"We can't fuck now..."

"We have 15 minutes..."

"Wayne... I can't..."

"Suck my dick..." Wayne said as he took his dick out his pants and started stroking it...

"Wayne! What if we get caught?"

"The sooner you start sucking..." he said as he pulled me close to him... "The sooner you won't have to worry..." he said as he put his hand on my shoulder... and I dropped down and put my mouth on his dick... "Yes... suck it..." Wayne growled as he grabbed my head and fucked my mouth...

"Mmmm...." I moaned and then I pulled my mouth off his dick and looked up at him... "Fuck my mouth Daddy..." I whispered and then I took his dick back in my mouth again...

"Ugh... Ugh... Ugh..." Wayne growled as he held my head with his hands and fucked my mouth. I could feel his body tensing up and I knew he was close so I grabbed his ass with both hands and pushed him down my throat... "Uuugggghhhh!" Wayne growled as he came in my mouth and I sucked and swallowed. "Mary..." he whispered...

"Yes Daddy?" I answered as I looked up at him...

"C'mere..." he said as he pulled me up into a kiss and held me...

"God I missed you..." I whispered...

"I missed you too..."

"Do we have a front porch?"

"Yes... Why?"

"Just thinking..." I sighed...

"I bet..."

"How much time do we have?"

"We need to go now..."

"Okay..." I sighed as we headed back to the station...

"Welcome back – we're getting ready to board – here's your bags..." the cashier said as she brought our bags out...

"Thank you..." Wayne said as he took the bags...

"Attention passengers – this is the final boarding call for the train to Ontario – please have your tickets and passports ready for boarding..."

"We're almost home!" I said...

"Yes we are..." Wayne said...

"Text me the picture we took at the falls..."

"Okay...." I sent the picture to Starr as soon as I got it...

"Aww... you look so happy..." she text me back...

"I am..." I text her back...

"Call me when you get home..."

"I will – I love you..."

"Love you too..."

"Did she get it?" Wayne asked...

"Yea... she got it..."

"What'd she say?"

"She said I look happy..."

"Tickets please..." the conductor said as we got closer to the train...

"Here ya go..." Wayne said as he handed the conductor the tickets and he tore off the stubs...

"Passports please..." the conductor said...

"Here ya go..." Wayne said as he handed the conductor the passports...

"License please..." the conductor said...

"Here ya go..." I said as I handed him my license...

"Have a nice trip..." the conductor said as he handed me my license and handed Wayne our passports...

"Thank you..." Wayne said before we got on the train and took our seats... "Mrs. Robinson?"

"Yes Mr. Robinson?"

"Will you have dinner with me tonight in the dining room?"

"Yes Mr. Robinson..."

"Wait here..." Wayne said as he got up...

"Where are you going?"

"To the bathroom..."

"Okay..." I looked out the window as Wayne went down the aisle...

"Excuse me – is there a sleeper car on this train?"

"Yes... why?" the conductor asked...

"Just wondering..."

"It's vacant if you want it – but you'll need to upgrade..."

"Can I borrow it?"

"Borrow it?" Aaahhhaaaaa... are you crazy?"

"I don't need the whole night – I just need an hour..."

"Man – you trying' to get me fired?"

"We just got married on Monday..."

"Oh wow – congratulations!"

"Thanks..."

"You need a whole hour?"

"I can make do with 30 minutes if I have to – I just wanna have a romantic dinner with my wife..."

"Le'me see what I can do..." the conductor said... "Go back to your seat – I'll come get you..."

"Okay – thanks..." Wayne said as he came back to sit down...

"Is everything okay?" I asked...

"Yea..." I snuggled down next to Wayne, wrapped his arm around me, and looked out the window until the sun went down...

"Hello Conrad..."

"Hello Bazil..."

"How's everything going?"

"They left Niagara Falls on schedule..."

"Any other activity?"

"He sent a picture from his cell phone..."

"And Mary?"

"She's been texting her daughter and posting in facebook..."

"Good..."

"We're just about ready to get started..."

"How long will the project take?"

"About an hour..."

"That's good... they won't be up all night..."

"Depends on them..."

"Keep me posted..."

"Will do..."

"Excuse me – I need you to come with me please..." the conductor said...

"Is everything okay?" I asked...

"Everything's fine – just come with me please..."

"Okay..." I said as I got up to follow the conductor and Wayne followed. We followed the conductor down the aisle where I saw Wayne go earlier and before I could ask what was going on, the conductor stopped me...

"In here please..." the conductor said as he opened the door to the sleep car...

"Wayne..." I whispered as I started to cry. The bed was positioned as a sofa and a table was set for two with a single blue rose in the center...

"Thank you..." Wayne said as the conductor winked at Wayne and walked away. Wayne came inside, closed the door, pushed me up against the door, and kissed me hard... "Mmmm.... Mmmm.... Mmmm...." I moaned as Wayne's hands were all over me, squeezing my ass, my back, my hips, and my breasts...

"I'm going to fuck the shit outta you..." Wayne breathed as he started kissing my neck and moved between my breasts...

"Wayne..." I whispered as he took my breasts out of my blouse and sucked my nipples wile squeezing them... "Wayne... huh..."

"Excuse me..." the conductor said as he knocked on the door. I hurried to the couch and Wayne opened the door...

"It's not much – but it's the best I can do – we closed the dining room on this car..." he said as he put two boxes on the table...

"Thank you..." Wayne said as he closed the door. Each box had a cheeseburger, a bag of potato chips, and a can of Pepsi. Steam was coming out the bag...

"Oh good – he heated them up..." I said as I picked up the burger, took the bag off it, and bit into it... "Oh my God – this is good – try it..." I said and then I took another bite. Wayne didn't say anything – he just watched me... "Wayne?"

What's wrong?" Wayne didn't answer me – he just moved closer to me and pulled me into a kiss...

"I love you..."

"I love you too..." I said and then I took another bite... "Now eat..."

"Okay..." he laughed as he took the wrapper off his cheeseburger and started eating...

"How y'all doin' in there?" the conductor asked...

"We're okay..." Wayne answered...

"Why does he keep checking on us like that?" I laughed...

"Because we're not supposed to be in here..."

"Ooohhh... we better hurry up then..."

"We better..." Wayne said as he pushed me down and unzipped my pants...

"Wayne... we can't..." Wayne took a napkin off the table, put it in my mouth, slid my pants down to my ankles, spread my legs, and dove in... "Uggghhh!" I moaned as Wayne grabbed my ass, held me against his mouth, and sucked my clit hard. My eyes rolled in back of my head as Wayne picked my ass up off the sofa and I rode his face... "Uggh! Uggh! Uggh!"

"Mmmm.... Yes Mommy... gimmie dat..." Wayne stuck his tongue inside me, pressed his nose against my clit, and I was done...

"Uuuuggghhhh! Uuuuggghhhh!" Wayne held my ass up and sucked my clit softly as my legs shook...

"Mmmm.... Damn Mommy... you taste so good... Mmmm..." Wayne put me back down on the sofa, pulled up my pants, sat me up, and saw tears in my eyes... "Mommy... did I hurt you?"

"No..." Wayne kissed my eyes, my tears, and my mouth... "Promise me you'll never leave me again..."

"I promise..." he said as he kissed me... "I'll never leave you... again..."

"We'll be there soon – I need to lock up..." the conductor said...

"Okay..." Wayne said as he got up and opened the door...

"I just need to get this table outta here, clean up a little, and then I can lock up..." The conductor said...

"Thanks for the burgers – they're really good..." I said as I picked up the chips and the sodas and we went back to our seats. The conductor smiled to himself as he saw the wet spot on the sofa.

# Chapter 15

"Hello Conrad..."
"Hello Bazil..."
"How's everything?"
"They just got started..."
"Glad to hear it..."

"Attention passengers – we'll be pulling into Ontario in about 15 minutes – please make sure you have everything and please make sure you have your passports ready when you leave the train – welcome to Ontario..."

"Oh my God! We're home!" I exclaimed...

"Yes... we're home..." Wayne said as he kissed me...

"I can't wait to go home... and go to bed... I'm tired..." I yawned...

"Not too tired... I hope..."

"We have an emergency!" the conductor said as he ran down to the engineer...

"What's wrong?"

"It's one of our passengers... well... both of them...

"What's wrong? Are they ill?"

"No..."

"What is it then?"

"The police will be waiting to take them into custody as soon as they get off the train!"

"Who?"

"The Robinsons..."

"The newlyweds?"

"Yea..."

"Aww damn...."

"Look Wayne – we're here!" I exclaimed as I got up out my seat...

'Okay... hang on a sec..." Wayne laughed as he got up and got our bags...

"I can't wait 'till the sun comes up – I wanna see everything Ontario has to offer...

"So do I..."

"Mr. & Mrs. Robinson?"

"Yes?" Wayne answered...

"I need you to come with me please..." the conductor said...

"Oh man – did you get in trouble?" Wayne whispered..."

"Naahh... it's cool – but I need you to come with me..."

"Okay..." Wayne said as we followed the conductor. When we got to the exit, I got really scared...

"Mr. & Mrs. Robinson?"

"Yes officer?" Wayne answered...

"May I see your passports?"

"Yes sir..." Wayne answered as he handed the officer our passports...

"Maam?"

"Yes officer?"

"May I see your ID?"

"Sure..." I said as I handed the officer my ID..."

"Okay – I need to hang on to these – ad I need you to come with us..."

"Is there a problem officer?" Wayne asked...

"We'll discuss it down at the station..." he answered as he opened the door to the squad car and I got it...

"Are we under arrest?"

"No..."

"Okay..." Wayne said as he got in the car. We rode down to the station without speaking. I took Wayne's hand and squeezed it...

"I'm scared..." Wayne took me in his arms and held me until we got to the station. When we got to the station the officer got out and opened the door for us...

"Please go inside and wait for me..." he said...

"Yes sir..." Wayne said as we went inside the station, sat on the bench in the lobby, and waited. The officer came inside and motioned for us to follow him down the hall so we followed him until we got to the end of the hallway and we all went into a room on the right...

"I'm Sergeant Gallagher..." he said as he closed the door...

"Okay..." Wayne said...

"Do you have an address here in Ontario?"

"Yes... we do..." Wayne answered...

"May I have your address?"

"Sure – it's "201 East Arrow Highway, Toronto, Ontario M1E4Y1..." Wayne answered...

"I'm sorry to inform you there was an explosion earlier this evening... your home was burned down..."

"Oh my God!" I exclaimed...

"What happened?" Wayne asked...

"Apparently someone was using a propane grill for their barbeque and didn't shut it off properly..."

"Wow..." Wayne said as he shook his head... "I just bought the property a few weeks ago..."

"Was your property insured?"

"Yes..."

"That's a good thing – once the adjusters do an investigation and determine there was no foul play – you'll get a check for the value of the property – in the meantime – you'll need to go to the shelter tonight..."

"Did you say the shelter?" I asked...

"You can go to a hotel if you like – but – depending on how much money you have –hotels are expensive – you could be displaced for two to three weeks..."

"Mary... I'm sorry..." Wayne said as he started crying...

"Wayne... this isn't your fault..." I said as I pulled him to me and he cried in my chest...

"I just wanted to make you happy..."

"Wayne... look at me..." Wayne lifted his head and I kissed his eyes, his tears, and his mouth... "I've been happy since the day you asked me to marry you..."

"I love you..."

"I love you too..."

"We can go back to Bridgeport if you want..."

"I don't want to go back to Bridgeport..."

"But we don't have anywhere else to live..."

"We'll figure something out..."

"Mary... I can't ask you to stay in the shelter with me..."

"And I can't leave my husband..."

"You'd be willing to stay with me?" Even if it means we have to go to a shelter?"

"Yes..."

"Wow... you must really love your husband..." Sergeant Gallagher said...

"I do..."

"You're a lucky man Mr. Robinson..."

"I know..."

"Well – I can take you to Good Shepard Ministries – they're open 24 hours – and they're the best shelter we have downtown – oh wait a minute – they only accept men – the Red Door Family Shelter would be better for you – but they're closed right now – and they don't open until 9 a.m...."

"Mary – we can't do this..." Wayne said as he took out his cellphone... "Yes – I need to report a claim..."

"Okay sir – how can I help you?"

"Our home was burned down tonight..."

"Oh my God – I'm so sorry – do you have anywhere to stay?"

"No..."

"I'm so sorry to hear that – did you call the fire department?"

"We're sitting at the police station in Ontario, Canada..."

"What happened sir?"

"We were on our way home – we just got off the train – we were brought here by Sergeant Gallagher..."

"Okay – go ahead..."

"He said someone was barbequing and didn't turn off their propane tank properly – and it exploded..."

"Okay sir – did you have a homeowner's policy?"

"Yes..."

"Okay – that's good – your policy covers a hotel... if you need it..."

"Yes please – thank you..."

"Okay – let me speak to Sergeant Gallagher..."

"Here..." Wayne said as he handed Sergeant Gallagher the phone...

"Hello? Uh huh... yes Maam... I can do that... sure... hang on..." he said as he took out a pen and pad... "Okay – go ahead... uh huh... got it – I'll get this right over to you..." he said as he got up, handed the phone back to Wayne, and left the room...

"Hello?"

"What's your name sir?"

"Wayne Robinson..."

"Mr. Robinson – I just spoke with Sergeant Gallagher – as soon as I receive a copy of your police report we'll get to work processing your claim – in the meantime – find a hotel – we'll pay up to $100 per night for 10 days  if you need more time we'll re-visit it..."

"How do I pay for the room?"

"You call the hotel – tell them you need a room for 10 days – then give them this claim number – ready?"

"Yea – I'm ready..."

"Okay – 14LZ0123..."

"That's it?"

"That's it – if you have any problems – call us back and give us the claim number..."

"What's your name?"

"My name is Lonnie..."

"Thank you Lonnie..."

"You're welcome Mr. Robinson – and remember – you're in good hands with Allstate..."

"Wayne – what's going on?" I asked...

"Allstate is going to start working on our claim as soon as they get a copy of the police report – and they'll pay up to $100 per night for a hotel for 10 days..."

"So... we don't have to go to a shelter?"

"No..."

"Oh thank God!"

"You're welcome..." God said...

"I knew you didn't want to go..."

"I was going to... for you..."

"I know – but now we don't have to – give me my laptop – let's find a hotel..." Wayne said...

"Okay..." I sighed as I gave Wayne the laptop and we started looking at hotels...

"Okay – let's stay here..." I said...

"Hmmmm... Auzre Hotel & Suites – three stars – 8.8 excellent rating – okay – I'll call them now..." Wayne said as he called the hotel...

"Thank you for calling Azure Hotel & Suites – may I make a reservation for you?"

"Yes – we need a room for 10 days – starting tonight..."

"Sure – let me see what we have available... okay sir – we have 3 rooms available – each comes with a king size bed and each room comes with free Wi-Fi and breakfast for two each day – how will you be paying for the room?"

"With my Allstate Insurance Policy..."

"Okay sir – may I have your claim number?"

"Yes – 14LZ0123..."

"Hold on please..."

"What's going on?" I asked...

"She put me on hold... yes – I'm here..."

"Okay Mr. Robinson – you're all set – you check in tonight and check out on Sunday, July 7th..."

"Thank you – we'll be there soon..."

"See you soon..."

"Everything okay?" Sergeant Gallagher asked as he came back in...

"Yes – we got a room at the Azure Hotel & Suites..." Wayne answered...

"Great – I sent everything over to your insurance company – I'll take you to the hotel..."

"Thank you Sergeant Gallagher..." we said in unison...

"Hello Conrad..."

"Hello Bazil..."

"How'd everything go?"

"The project's completed..."

"Nice..."

"He's been using his phone..."

"Okay..."

"She'll probably call her daughter soon..."

"Im sure she will..."

"Good night Bazil..."

"Good night Conrad..."

"Welcome to Azure – are you checking in?"

"Yes – I'm Mr. Robinson..."

"Mr. Robinson – we've been expecting you – I just need you to sign here – this states that you're responsible for any damages and it also states that you understand there's an additional charge of $250 for smoking in the room..."

"Okay..." Wayne said as he took the forms and signed them...

"Here's your room keys – you'll be in room 215 on the 2nd floor..."

"Thank you..." Wayne said as he took my hand and we went to the elevator... "Are you going to call Starr?"

"Yea..."

"What's wrong?"

"Nothing..."

"You don't want to call her?"

"I don't want her to worry..."

"Just tell her we're here – we're tired – and we're going to bed..."

"Okay... I'll do that..." I said as Wayne opened the door and pulled me into the room...

"Oh wow – it's beautiful..." I whispered...

"You're beautiful..." Wayne whispered as he kissed me...

"Oh Wayne..." I moaned as he started kissing my neck...

"Yes Mommy..."

"You said something... about fucking the shit outta me..."

"Yes... I did..."

"Let's get to bed..."

"Okay..." Wayne said as we ripped our clothes off and dropped them to the floor...

"Come with me Mommy..." he said as he took my hand and led me to the bed...

"Yes Daddy..." I said as I pulled back the covers, got in the bed, and spread my legs. Wayne got on the bed, got on top of me, eased himself inside me, and put his tongue in my mouth as he started thrusting...

"Mmmph... Mmmph... Mmmph... Mmmph..."

"Hmmph... Hmmph... Hmmph... Hmmph..."

"What's wrong?" Chandler asked...

"She won't answer her phone!" Starr snapped...

"Starr?"

"Yes Chandler?"

"They left early this morning – they rode all day – they probably went straight to bed…"

"You're right…"

"Send her a text…" he said as he went up behind her… "Tell her you love her…" he said as he kissed her neck… "Put down your phone…" he said as he turned her around to face him… "And let me make love to you…" he said as he kissed her…

"Mmmm…. Never mind…" she said as she threw her arms around Chandler's neck, threw her legs around him, and he carried her into the bedroom.

# Chapter 16

"Good morning Mrs. Robinson..." Wayne said as he kissed me awake...

"Good morning Mr. Robinson..."

"Let's go get breakfast..."

"Can't we have room service?"

"We could – but if we go to the dining room we won't be charged...

"Okay..." I sighed... "I'll get up..." Wayne and I quickly threw on our clothes, grabbed our phones, and went to the dining room... "This is actually pretty nice..." I said...

"It is nice..." Wayne agreed.

"Let's pick a table..." I said...

"That one – by the window..." Wayne said as he pointed to the table and we went to sit down... "Wait here – I'll be back..."

"Okay..." I sighed. I smiled as I watched Wayne making us coffee. Wayne came back to the table with the coffee and set it on the table... "Thank you..."

"You're welcome – I'll go get us something to eat..." Wayne said as he went back over to the station, made us plates, and came back to the table...

"I love you..."

"I love you too..." Wayne said as we ate...

"This food's really good — almost like we ordered room service..."

"It is — and so's the coffee..."

"Oh shoot — Starr's calling me..."

"Answer it..."

"Okay..." I sighed...

"Hi Starr..."

"Hi Mommy! I miss you!"

"I miss you too — are you at work?"

"I'm not going in today — why didn't you call me last night?"

"We got in late — we were so tired — we went straight to bed..."

"That's what Chandler said...

"Starr — we're having breakfast — I'll call you back when we're done..."

"Okay Mommy — I love you..."

"I love you too..."


"Feel better now?" Chandler asked...

"No..."

"No? Why?"

"Mommy just lied to me..."

"Starr! What would she have to lie about?"

"I don't know... yet..."


"Mary?"

"I know Wayne... I know..."

"Mary..." Wayne said as he took my hand...

"I just wanna finish breakfast..."

"Okay – but when we get upstairs you're gonna call her back – and you're gonna tell her..."

"Okay, okay..." I sighed. We finished our coffee and breakfast without speaking.

"She'll be fine – she has Chandler..."

"I know... it's just..."

"I'm gonna get us some more coffee... c'mon..." Wayne said as he waited for me to get up. Wayne took my hand and we walked over to the station, got more coffee, got in the elevator, and went back to the room. As soon as Wayne closed the door, he took the coffee out my hand, put it on the table, and pulled me into a kiss... "I'm right here..."

"I know..." I said as I sat down at the table, started drinking my coffee, and called Starr..."

"Hi Mommy..."

"Hi Starr..."

"Are you okay Mommy?"

"Is Chandler there?"

"Yes Mommy – Chandler's here – why?"

"When we got here last night – we had to go to the police station..."

"Why Mommy?"

"There was a fire..."

"Oh my God! Are you okay?"

"Starr – don't cry..."

"Mary – it's Chandler – what happened?"

"There was a fire – someone was having a barbeque they didn't shut off their propane tank – it exploded – our house burned down..."

"Are you okay?"

"We're fine – Wayne has homeowner's insurance – they're covering the hotel..."

"Where are you staying?"

"We're at the Azure Hotel & Suites – it's a very nice hotel..."

"Do you need us to come up to Canada?"

"Chandler – that's very sweet – but we're okay - I promise..."

"Le'me speak to Wayne..."

"Here..." I said as I handed Wayne the phone...

"Hello Chandler..."

"Y'all good? Really?"

"Yes Chandler – we're fine..."

"If you need anything – call us – okay?"

"Yes Chandler..."

"What'd the insurance company say?"

"They're working on my claim now – they've been very responsive – Sergeant Gallagher made sure they got the paperwork and he brought us to the hotel..."

"Gimmie his number – never mind – I'll look it up..."

"Chandler – we're fine..."

"I heard you – but I'ma speak to Sergeant Gallagher anyway..."

"Okay Chandler – could you put Starr on the phone please?"

"Here Starr – Wayne wants to talk to you..."

"Hello?"

"Starr – we're fine..."

"I knew something was wrong – I felt it..."

"Starr - your mother doesn't want you to worry about her..."

"I can't help it..."

"Starr – I love your mother – I won't let anything happen to her – I promise..."

"Okay – can I speak to Mommy?"

"Sure – here Mary..."

"Starr – are you okay?"

"I'm okay... I just want you to be okay – when you said there was a fire I got scared..."

"I know... but I'm fine..."

"I know..."

"Starr – don't tell your father... okay?"

"Okay Mommy – you'll call me – right?"

"Yes Starr – I'll call you - I promise..."

"Mommy?"

"Yes Starr?"

"You can come back if you need to..."

"That's very sweet Starr... thank you..."

"You're welcome – I love you Mommy..."

"I love you too – now I need you to take care of yourself... and my grandchild..."

"Okay Mommy..."

"I'll talk to you soon..."

"Okay Mommy..." Starr said as she hung up...

"I see why you didn't want to call her..."

"Yea..."

"Thank God Chandler's with her – he's a good guy..."

"Yes... he is..."


"I knew it!"

"Starr – calm down... they're fine..."

"I felt it..."

"Starr..." Chandler said as he pulled her into a hug... "They're fine..."

"I was so scared..."

"I know..."

"I can't lose Mommy Chandler..."

"Starr – you're not going to lose your mother – she's fine – she has her husband..."

"I'm glad he married Mommy..."

"You are?"

"Yea... he really loves her..."

"I'ma call Sergeant Gallagher and make sure everything's okay..."

"Thank you Chandler..." she said as she looked up at him...

"You don't have to thank me – I told you when we got married – your parents are important to you – they're important to me..."

"Mommy doesn't want me to tell Daddy..."

"I agree..."

"You do?"

"Yea..."

"Me too..."

"I'ma make us some coffee – then I'ma call Sergeant Gallagher..." Chandler said as he went into the kitchen to make coffee...

"Toronto Police – how may I help you?"

"This is Sergeant Corbett from the Bridgeport Police Department – may I speak to Sergeant Gallagher?"

"Sure Sergeant Corbett – may I tell him what this is in reference to?"

"I need the police report on the Robinsons..."

"I can get you the report – but I need to ask you..."

"They're my wife's parents..." Chandler interrupted...

"Oh my goodness – sorry Sergeant – I'll get the report to you asap – do you still need to speak with Sergeant Gallagher?"

"Yes Maam..."

"Okay – one moment..."

"Sergeant Corbett – this is Sergeant Gallagher – what can I do for you?"

"The Robinsons are my wife's parents..."

"Oh my goodness – she must be worried sick..."

"She is..."

"They're fine – thank God they weren't here when the explosion happened..."

"Exactly..."

"It was really irresponsible of them to have their propane tank on like that – thank God no one was hurt..."

"Thank you for taking care of them and getting them to the hotel..."

"You're welcome – if there are any other developments I'll keep you posted..."

"Any other developments?"

"It's nothing – the insurance company just needs to investigate and make sure it was an accident..."

"You don't think..."

"Oh no..." Sergeant Gallagher interrupted – they were nowhere near the explosion – it's just procedure..."

"Have you seen this before?"

"I've seen it all Sergeant..."

"Well – hopefully their insurance company will process their claim quickly so they can get outta the hotel and into their home..."

"I hope so – listen – I gotta go – I'll keep you posted..."

"Thank ya Sergeant..." Chandler said as he hung up...

"Good morning Conrad..."

"Good morning Bazil..."

"How's everything?"

"Your son-in-law is asking questions..."

"Will he get any answers?"

"A few..."

"Should I be worried?"

"Naa..."

"Starr?"

"Yes Chandler?"

"Come in the kitchen..." Starr come into the kitchen, went over to Chandler, threw her arms around him, and kissed him... "Mmmm.... I like that..." he said as he pulled her close to him and held her...

"What else do you like?" Starr asked as she started kissing his neck...

"I like that too..." Chandler breathed...

"How 'bout this?" she asked as she loosened his robe, took his dick in her hand, and started stroking it...

"Oh yea... I... like... that..." Starr held Chandler, put her head in his chest, and continued stroking him... "Starr..." Chandler moaned as he grabbed her around her waist, held her tighter, and moaned... "Huh... Huh... Huh... Huh..." Starr's hand was coated in pre-cum and she used it to continue stroking Chandler's dick as he grabbed her face and put his tongue in her mouth... "Mmmph... Mmmph... Mmmph... Mmmph..." Chandler reached down between Starr's legs, spread her lips with his fingers, and started rubbing her clit...

"Hmmmph... Hmmmph... Hmmmph... Hmmmph... Hmmmph..."

"Mmmph... Mmmph... Mmmph... Mmmph... Mmmmppphhh!" Chandler came in her hand as he pushed his fingers inside her pussy...

"Huh... Huh... Huh... Huh..."

"That's it... come for me... come on my hand..."

"Haa.... Haa... Haa... Haa... Haa... Haaaa...!" Chandler took his fingers out her pussy and put them in her mouth and she sucked them. Chandler waited until she was done and then he kneeled down between her legs, spread her lips, and started licking and sucking her clit... "Chandler... it's sensitive..." she moaned as her legs shook. Chandler put one leg up on his shoulder, put his tongue inside her, and continued sucking... "Chandler... Ooohhh..." Chandler took his tongue out her pussy and began swirling it around her clit... "Chandler... Huh... Huh..." Chandler held Starr as she started trembling... "Huh... Huh... Huuuuhhhhh!" Chandler continued licking softly until Starr tapped him on his shoulder. Chandler looked up at Starr, stood up, kissed her, and put his tongue in her mouth...

"That's not fair..." she breathed...

"Excuse me?"

"I didn't get to do you..."

"You wanna do me?"

"Yes..." she breathed as she knelt down, grabbed Chandler's ass, and took his dick in her mouth all the way down to his balls, took it out, and took it back in again...

"Starr... Fuck!" Chandler moaned as he grabbed her head with both hands and let her control the pace...

"Mmmm... Mmmm... Mmmm..." she moaned as she sucked. Chandler looked down and was so turned on watching her enjoy herself. Starr looked up at Chandler and saw him watching her so she took his dick in her hand, swirled her tongue around it, and suck the head while simultaneously stroking him...

"Starr... Fuck... I'm cumming... I'm cumming... Uuuggghhh!" Star swallowed and continued sucking until his dick went limp in her mouth and then she stood up...

"Starr..." Chandler breathed as he pulled her into a kiss...

"Where... did... you... learn... that?" Starr stopped kissing Chandler and turned her head away... "Starr?"

"Yes Chandler?"

"Look at me..." he said as he picked up her head by her chin... "What's wrong?"

"Nothing..."

"Tell me..."

"I... watched it..."

"You watched it?"

"Yea..."

"That's sweet..."

"You're not mad?"

"Why would I be mad?"

"Because... it's private..."

"Come here..." Chandler said as he took Starr by the hand and led her into the bedroom... "Sit down..."

"Okay..." Starr watched as Chandler turned on the television and turned to Cinemax... "Chandler..."

"Sshhh..." Chandler said as he sat down beside her and kissed her... "We can watch it together..."

"Chandler?'

"Yes Starr?"

"How long have you..."

"Watched porn?"

"Yea..."

"Starr – I've been watching porn for years..."

"Years?"

"I used to watch it at my sister's house..."

"You did?"

"Yea...."

"I never watched it..."

"Never? Why?"

"I was afraid my mother would catch me..." she laughed...

"We can watch it anytime you want..."

"What if I want to watch it all the time?"

"We can..."

"I'd like that..."

"So would I..."

"I need some coffee..."

"Sorry about that — you'da had your coffee earlier if you didn't start..." Chandler laughed...

"You're the one that started it!" Starr laughed...

"Me? How?"

"You said you liked it when I kissed you!"

"Okay — so who asked me what else I liked?"

'Me..."

"So... whose fault was it?"

"Yours!" Starr laughed...

"How is it my fault?"

"Because..." she said as she got up off the bed, pushed his legs apart, stood between them, and kissed him... "You made me fall in love with you..."

"Starr... I love you..."

"I love you too..."

"Keep it up... you gon' mess around and wind up on your back..." Chandler laughed as he grabbed her...

"Okay... okay..." she laughed as he tickled her...

"You gon' stop? Huh?"

"Yes! I'll stop!" she laughed...

"C'mon..." he said as he got up and took her hand... "I have a surprise for you..."

"Okay!" she squealed as she followed him into the kitchen...

"Sit down..." Chandler said. Starr watched as Chandler took two cups out the cabinet, put them on the counter, and made them coffee. Chandler put the coffee in front of Starr, put a cup in front of himself, and started drinking his coffee...

"Chandler?"

"Yes Starr?"

"You said you had a surprise for me?"

"Drink your coffee Starr..." he said as he smiled...

"Okay..." Starr watched Chandler intently as he finished his coffee, put his cup down, and turned to look at her...

"Starr?"

"Yes Chandler?"

"I need to you to call Amy and tell her you have a family emergency..."

"Okay – why?"

"We're leaving tomorrow..."

"We are?"

"We're going to see your parents..."

"Oh my God! Chandler! Thank you! Thank you! Thank you!" she squealed as she grabbed

Chandler into a hug and started jumping up and down...

"Alright Starr... you gon' mess around and get me started again..." Chandler laughed...

"I love you... I love you... I love you..." Starr said as she kissed Chandler over and over and over..."

"Starr... stop..."

"Okay – I'm sorry – I can't help it..."

"I need you to call Amy..."

"Okay – I'll call Amy..."

"I'ma call my job – I'll make us breakfast – then we need to get ready..."

"Okay Chandler..."

"We'll be gone for about a week – I won't know for sure until we get there..."

"Okay..." Starr said as she called Amy...

"Hello Starr..."

"Amy – I can't come back to work..."

"You don't like it here?"

"Oh no – I'm sorry – I have a family emergency..."

"What happened?"

"My mother..."

"Oh my God – is she okay?"

"She's okay..."

"Oh thank God – what happened?"

"There was a fire..."

"Oh Starr – I'm sorry..."

"They're staying in a hotel..."

"They don't have anywhere to go?"

"No..."

"I understand – I'd go check on my mother too..."

"You're not mad?"

"Of course not – how long will you be gone?"

"Chandler says maybe a week he says he won't know for sure until we get there..."

"Your husband's a good man..."

"Yes... he is..."

"Have you talked to your mother?"

"Yes..."

"How did she sound?"

"She's more worried about me than I am about her..."

"Oh that's good – that means she's okay..."

"Thank you Amy..."

"For what?"

"You always make me feel better..."

"Aww... you're very sweet..."

"So are you..."

"Okay – you call me and let me know what's going on okay?"

"I will Amy..."

"Okay – good luck..." Amy said as she hung up...

"Yea Sarge?" the dispatcher answered...

"I have a family emergency – I need to head out to Ontario..."

"Canada?"

"Yes..."

"What happened?"

"My wife's parents – their house was in a fire..."

"Are they okay?"

"They're homeless…"

"Oh damn – sorry to hear that – I'll send the paperwork over to be processed – keep us posted Sarge…"

"I will – did you get the police report?"

"Yea Sarge – we got it…"

"Okay – I'm leaving tomorrow morning – I'll keep you posted…"

"Hello Conrad…"

"We might have a problem…"

"What happened?"

"Your son-in-law is leaving for Ontario tomorrow morning…"

"Shit!"

# Chapter 17

Chandler and Starr slept through the morning on the train. Starr woke up first... "Chandler..." she whispered...

"Yes Starr?" Chandler yawned...

"Where are we?"

"I'm not sure..." he answered as he sat up..."

"I'm hungry..."

"I'll go get us something to eat — wait here..." Chandler said as he got up...

"I wanna go with you..."

"Okay — c'mon..." Chandler said as he headed to the dining room and Starr followed...

"This is kinda nice..." Starr said...

"What can I getcha?" the conductor asked...

"Whatcha got?" Chandler asked...

"We got burgers, hot dogs, chicken, chips, pretzels, soda, and beer..."

"Okay — le'me git two cheeseburgers, a Pepsi, a Heineken, and two bags of chips..."

"You got it..." the conductor said as he put the burgers in the microwave. The conductor put two boxes on the counter, took the burgers out the microwave, put the chips, the soda, and the

Heineken in the box, and turned to Chandler... "That'll be $18.00..."

"Here ya go..." Chandler said as he handed the conductor a $20 bill and they went back to their seats...

"Hmmm... this is actually good..." Starr said as she ate...

"It is..." Chandler agreed. They finished their food and looked out the window until the conductor made an announcement...

"Attention passengers – we'll be approaching Niagara Falls shortly – please have your tickets out and your passports ready. Everyone got up to leave and waited for the train to pull into Niagara Falls. When it was their turn to get off, the conductor stopped them...

"Tickets please..."

"Here ya go..." Chandler said as he handed him the tickets...

"Passports please..."

"Here ya go..." Chandler said as he handed the conductor the passports...

"We leave for Toronto in about an hour – be back here by 5:45 p.m. sharp for boarding. Chandler went over to the window to see the cashier...

"Can we leave our bags here?" Chandler asked...

"Yes sir – just make sure you're back here at 5:45 p.m...."

"Thank ya Maam..." Chandler said as he gave her the bags...

"C'mon Chandler — let's go down by the falls..." Starr said as she pulled Chandler by the hand...

"Okay... I'm comin'..." Chandler laughed as they ran towards the falls...

"I wanna take some selfies..." Starr said as she took out her phone and set up the camera..."

"Gimmie that..." Chandler said as he held the phone up, set the time, pointed it at them, and kissed her so the phone took the photo...

"Oh Chandler... look..." Starr breathed as the light began changing colors in the falls...

"It's beautiful..." Chandler said as he held Starr in his arms...

"Now I see why my mother wants to live here..." Starr breathed...

"I wonder if anybody got caught having sex over there?" Chandler asked as he pointed to the bushes...

"Chandler... No..."

"C'mon..." Chandler breathed in her ear as he massaged her breasts...

"Chandler... we'll get caught..."

"We'll go on the other side... where the tree is..."

"I'm scared..."

"I know..." Chandler said as he took Starr by the hand and led her behind the bushes...

"Chandler..."

"Ssshhh..." he said as he pulled her close to him and whispered in her ear... "I'ma lay down in the grass — I'ma take my dick out my pants —

you lift your skirt – you sit on my dick – and if anybody comes, you just stop – okay?"

"Okay..." she breathed. Chandler laid down in the grass, took his dick out his pants, and waved it at Starr. Starr raised her skirt, slid her panties over, and sat on his dick... "Damn your pussy feels good..." Chandler breathed as he grabbed her waist and pushed himself up inside her...

"Chandler..." Starr moaned as she began riding his dick...

"Yes... that's it... ride my dick..." Chandler breathed as he grabbed her ass...

"Chandler... huh... huh..."

"Come for me Starr..."

"Okay..." she moaned as she started riding his dick harder...

"Yes... ride my dick Starr... gimmie that pussy..." Chandler growled as he pushed her down on his dick and her clit rubbed against his pelvis...

"Ohh... Ooohhh Ooohh... Chandler... Chandler..."

"That's it... ride my dick..." Chandler watched Starr's face as she threw her head back and her body shook...

"I'm cumming... I'm cumming... I'm cumming..."

"Uggh! Uggh! Uggh! Uggh! Uggh!" Starr's breathing slowed down and she laid down on Chandler and kissed him...

"What is good?"

"Yea... it was good..."

"Let's get up before we get caught..."

"Okay..." Starr breathed as she got up and stood up. Chandler put his dick in his pants, fixed himself, and stood up behind Starr...

"I just thought of something..." Starr laughed...

"What's that?"

"I wonder if my mother... and Wayne..."

"Ask her..."

"No!" she laughed...

"You're the one that wanna know..." Chandler laughed...

"Do you think they did?"

"Probably..."

"What time is it?"

"It's about 5:30..."

"Let's go back..."

"I wanna take another picture..."

"Okay..."

"This is the after picture..." Chandler said as he held Starr, positioned the phone, set the timer, and took the picture...

"Le'me see..." she said...

"See how beautiful you are?"

"Chandler..."

"That's your orgasmic glow..."

"My what?"

"Every time you have an orgasm... you glow... and it's beautiful..." Chandler said as he kissed her...

"Chandler..." she whispered as her eyes filled with tears...

"I love you..." he said as he kissed her eyes and her mouth...

"I love you too..."

"Let's go back inside..." he said as he wrapped his arm around her and they walked arm in arm back to the station. After they boarded the train and took their seats, Chandler held Starr and they looked out the window until they heard the following announcement...

"Attention passengers – we'll be pulling into Ontario in about 15 minutes – please make sure you have everything and please make sure you have your passports ready when you leave the train – welcome to Ontario..." When it was there turn to get off the conductor stopped them...

"Ticket's please..."

"Here ya go..." Chandler said as he handed him the tickets...

"Passports please..."

"Here ya go..." Chandler said as he handed the conductor the passports...

"You're all set – welcome to Ontario..." the conductor said as they stepped off the train and they were stopped again by an officer...

"Passports please..."

"Sergeant Gallagher?" Chandler asked...

"Yes sir – who are you?"

"I'm Sergeant Corbett – and this is my wife – Starr..."

"I see – its nice meeting you in person – but you've made an unnecessary trip..."

"Unnecessary?"

"Sergeant – you don't have any jurisdiction here..."

"Sergeant Gallagher – I'm not here to interfere with your investigation – I just want to take my wife to see her parents..."

"That's fine – I just need your ID's so I can verify your information – once I verify your information I'll take you to the hotel...

"Okay..." Chandler said as they got in the squad car and waited...

"Everything checks out – I'll take you over to the hotel now..." Sergeant Gallagher said...

"Thank you Sergeant Gallagher..." Starr said...

"You're welcome – you have nice parents..."

"Thank you..."

"They're lucky to have you..."

"I'm lucky to have them..."

"Do they know you're here?"

"No..."

"Oh wow – it'll be a nice surprise..." he said as he parked the car...

"We're here?" Starr asked...

"You're here..." Sergeant Gallagher said. They got out the car and Chandler spoke...

"How's everything going?"

"With the investigation?"

"Yea..."

"Everything's fine – you don't have to worry..."

"Thank you Sergeant Gallagher..."

"Call me Chris..."

"Thank you Chris..."

"You're welcome – call me if you need anything..."

"I will – thanks again..." Chandler said as they went into the hotel...

"Welcome to Azure Hotel & Suites – are you checking in?"

"Yes we are..." Chandler said...

"Name please?"

"Chandler Corbett..."

"Hello Mr. Corbett –your reservation is paid in full – we just need a credit card for incidentals – and we need you to sign this form stating that you understand there's a charge of $250 for smoking in the room..."

"Okay – here..." Chandler said as he gave the woman his credit card and signed the form...

"Thank you Mr. Corbett – I see you'll be checking out July 7th?"

"Yes Maam..."

"Here's your keys – you're in room 315 – if you need anything just call the front desk..."

"Thank you – c'mon Starr..." Chandler said as they went to the elevator...

"I can't wait to see Mommy..."

"Can you wait until tomorrow?"

"Yes... why?"

"I'm ready to go to bed..." Chandler said as he smiled at Starr mischievously.  They got off on the third floor, went to their room, and opened the door...

"Oh Chandler... this is nice!"

"I can be nicer..." he said as he put the do not disturb sign on the door, closed the door, dropped the bas, went up behind Starr, held her, and kissed her neck...

"Ooooohhh... I love it when you're nice to me..."

"Take your clothes off..." Chandler commanded. Starr took off her clothes and stood there naked in front of Chandler. She watched intently as Chandler took his clothes off and stood in front of her. "Get in the bed..." Chandler commanded. Starr pulled back the covers and got in the bed. Chandler got in the bed beside her, reached for the remote, and turned on the television. Chandler scanned the menu until he found what he was looking for... and then he turned it on...

"Oh yes... yes... fuck me..." she moaned on screen...

"She is so fake..." Starr laughed...

"What makes you say that?" Chandler laughed...

"They just got started — she's not even doing anything but laying there — she's just acting..." Starr laughed...

"You know that's their job — right?" Chandler laughed...

"I know — but at least act like you love him or something — grab his ass!" Starr laughed...

"Oh so you're a director now!" Chandler laughed...

"I'm just saying — people don't just wanna see sex — they wanna see love..."

"How 'bout that?" Chandler said as he pointed to the television...

"Oh now that's interesting..." she said as she watched the woman sucking the man's dick...

"Do you think she's enjoying that?"

"Yea..."

"Do you enjoy it?"

"Yea..."

"Oh yea?"

"Yea..."

"Tell me what you like about it..." Chandler breathed in her ear as he took her hand and placed it on his dick...

"I like how you feel... in my mouth..."

"Mmmm..." Chandler moaned as she stroked his dick... "What else?"

"I like that I make you feel good..."

"Mmmm... what else?"

"I like when you come..."

"You do?"

"Yea..."

"How 'bout that?" Chandler asked as he pointed to the television..."

"Yes..." Starr moaned...

"You like when I do that to you?" he asked as he put his hand between her legs and started rubbing her clit...

"Yes..." she moaned...

"I love doing that to you..."

"Ooohhh..."

"I love it when you get wet..."

"Ooohhh..."

"I love how you taste..." he breathed as he put two fingers inside her...

"Ooohhh... Ooohhh..."

"and... I love when you come..."

"Chandler... huh..."

"Spread your legs..." Chandler said as he pushed his fingers in deeper...

"Chandler... Chandler..."

"Your hand feels good on my dick..."

"Chandler... huh... Chandler..."

"Not yet..." Chandler breathed as he stopped what he was doing...

"Chandler... please..."

"That's what I wanna hear..."

"You want me to beg?"

"Yes..."

"Please..." she breathed as she pulled him on top of her and kissed him...

"Yes... Starr..."

"Please..." she breathed as she spread her legs wide, grabbed Chandler's ass with both hands, and pushed him inside her...

"Yes... Starr..." Chandler breathed as he kissed her...

"Please Chandler..." she breathed as she lifted her legs up and wrapped her legs around his back...

"Please... what?"

"Fuck me..."

"I didn't hear you..." he teased...

"Please... fuck me!"

"Okay..." he said as he turned up the volume on the television... and started thrusting slowly... "I want you to watch them while I fuck you..."

"Okay..." Starr breathed...

"And I want you to come... when she comes..." Chandler breathed as he started thrusting harder...

"Chandler... Chandler... Chandler..."

"Oh yes... fuck me... harder..." the woman screamed on the television...

"Your pussy's really wet – this is turning you on – isn't it?"

"Yes... Chandler... Yes..."

"Keep watching them..." Chandler breathed as he thrust even harder...

"Oh God! Fuck me! I'm coming! I'm coming!" the woman screamed...

"Chandler... Huh... Huh..."

"Do you think she's enjoying that?"

"Yes Chandler... yes..."

"Are you enjoying it?"

"Yes... huh... yes..."

"Show me..." Chandler growled in her ear as he fucked her harder...

"Aaahhh... Aaahhh... Aaahhh... Aaahh... Aaaaahhhhh!"

"What are they doing now?"

"He's fucking her from behind..." Starr breathed...

"Get up on your knees... and keep watching..." Starr got up on her knees and positioned herself so she could see what they were doing on the television... "You like this?"

Chandler breathed as he grabbed her hips and eased himself inside her...

"Yes Chandler... Huh..."

"Do you think he's enjoying it?"

"Yes Chandler..."

"Do you think I'm enjoying it?"

"Yes Chandler!" Starr moaned as Chandler started slapping up against her ass...

"I'm gonna do to you whatever he does to her..."

"Oh yes... fuck me... I'm coming again..." the woman screamed...

"You wanna come again?" Chandler asked...

"Yes Chandler... yes..."

"Keep watching..."

"Oh Chandler... Fuck... I'm cumming..."

"Give it to me Starr..."

"Aaahhh... Aaahhh... Aaahhh... Aaaahhh..." Chandler slammed his dick in her harder as her body shook...

"Yes Starr... come all over my dick!"

"Uggh! Uggh! Uggh! Uggh! Uggh!" the man moaned on the television...

"Uggh! Uggh! Uggh! Uggh! Uggh!" Chandler moaned... and then... just as Starr watched the man on television pull his dick out the woman's pussy and come in her mouth... Chandler did the same thing... "Starr! Fuck! Suck it!" Starr jerked Chandler's dick in her hand just like the woman on the television and when Chandler shot in her mouth, she let some dribble down her chin just like the woman on the television. Chandler closed his eyes, threw his head back, held Starr's head in his hands, and let Starr suck his dick as long as she wanted until she stopped... "C'mere..." he breathed and then he pulled her up into a kiss, tasting himself on her mouth and chin...

"Like that?" Starr breathed...

"Hell yea..." Chandler breathed... "Just like that..."

"Chandler..."

"Yes... Starr..."

"That was so good..."

"You like watching..."

"Yes..."

"So do I..."

"You were really hard..."

"And you were really wet..."

"Can we do it again?"

"Lay down on your back..."

"Okay..."

"I want you to watch him eat her pussy... while I eat yours..."

"Okay..." she breathed as she watched television... "Chandler... Huh... Huh..." Starr watched as the man spread the woman's legs on the television and jumped as Chandler did the same thing to her simultaneously...

"Ooohhh... Ooohhh... Ooohhh..." the woman moaned on the television as her ass rose up off the bed... and Starr also rose up off the bed. Chandler held Starr up off the bed as he licked and sucked her clit and Starr began moaning with the woman on the television...

"Oooohhh... Ooohhh... Ooohhh..."

"Yes... Yes... Yes..." Starr didn't take her eyes off the television as the man grabbed the woman's legs, pulled her to his face, and devoured her and Chandler did the same thing...

"Chandler! Chandler! Chandler! I'm cumming! I'm cumming!" the woman on the television was also screaming...

"Yes! Oh God! Right there! Don't stop!" the man on the television didn't stop and neither did Chandler as Starr's entire body shook along with the woman's body on the television...

"Haaa... Haaa... Haaa.... Aaaahhhhgh!" the woman on the television moaned along with Starr and it was music to Chandler's ears... and a delight to his mouth...

"Chandler... wait..." Chandler licked and sucked softer but he didn't stop... "Chandler... wait..." Chandler ignored her as he continued licking and slurping... "Chandler... wait... its sensitive..." Chandler stopped licker her clit, stuck his tongue inside her, and continued sucking...

"Mmmm... Mmmm... Mmmm..." Chandler moaned. Starr laid back, succeeded defeat, and let Chandler suck the juices out her pussy until he was content... and then he came up from between her legs and kissed her...

"Mmmm...." she moaned...

"Exactly..."

"Huh?"

"When you're really excited... you come hard... you taste good... and I want it..."

"You must've been really excited too..."

"I was..."

"You came a lot..."

"I know..."

"It ran out my mouth..."

"Just like our wedding night..."

"I'm glad you were ready for bed..."

"Me too..."

"Let's get up early..."

"Why?"

"So you can fuck me like you did in the squad car before you went to work..." she yawned as Chandler turned off the television and they went to sleep.

# <u>Twisted Mary Tree</u>

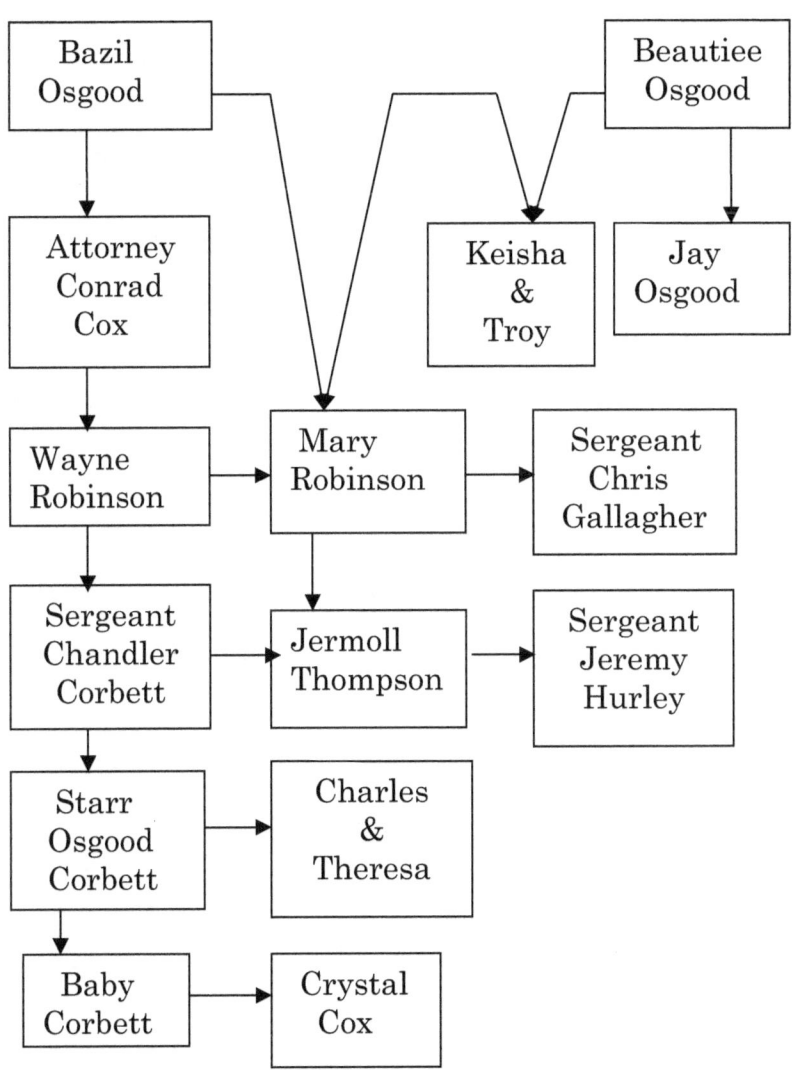